Lydia

A NOVEL

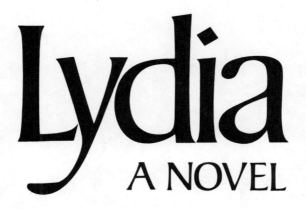

Lydia
A NOVEL

Lois T. Henderson

CHRISTIAN HERALD BOOKS
Chappaqua, New York

Library of Congress Cataloging in Publication Data
Henderson, Lois T.
  Lydia: a novel.

  1. Lydia (Biblical character)—Fiction. I. Title.
PZ4.H51124Ly [PS3558.E486] 813'.5'4 79-50946
ISBN 0-915684-32-2

First Edition
CHRISTIAN HERALD BOOKS, 40 Overlook Drive, Chappaqua, New York 10514
Printed in the United States of America

In loving memory
of my parents,
John R. and Freda Thompson

Preface

I want to express my deep appreciation to the people who did so much to help me with this book: Gladys Donaldson, who read and reread each chapter and offered many helpful suggestions; Ruth Curry, who typed the manuscript; Dikran Hadidian, Helen Tussey and Peg Wilson, librarians, who helped me find the books I needed for my research; and Pastor Robert C. Wilson, who offered suggestions when I encountered theological problems.

I believe *Lydia* needs a short word of explanation. I have tried, as much as possible, to adhere closely to the few scenes described in Acts, but I have taken liberties with names which do not appear in Acts but which are found in Paul's Letter to the Philippians. There is no scriptural indication that the Epaphroditus named in Philippians is related to Lydia, nor is there any suggestion that the jailer and Clement are the same man. But my imagination tells me that the relationship *may* have occurred, and that a converted jailer could have meant so much to Paul that he would send greetings years later.

Scholars have also suggested several physical ailments which might have been Paul's "thorn in the flesh." For the sake of this story I have accepted the idea that he may have been a hunchback. I have also provided a somewhat embellished version of the dramatic scene in prison in view of the overall development of this fictional account.

part one

...a certain woman named Lydia, from the city of Thyatira, a seller of purple, a worshipper of God... and...a certain slave-girl having a spirit of divination who was bringing her masters much profit by fortune-telling.

Acts 16:14a, 16b

1

The calendar and her son's predictions had told Lydia this would be an auspicious day. But there was nothing auspicious about the way her heart hammered in her throat as she made her way along the Via Egnatia, the street that dipped steeply toward the center of town.

She tried to calm herself, but fear was like a separate pulse in her body. She finally forced herself to stop and stand quietly under a clump of trees that shadowed the edge of the road. A slight gesture of her hand brought the slave who followed her to a discreet halt a short distance away. From where she stood Lydia could look out over the town of Philippi and the plain stretching toward Mount Symbolum. Beyond the cone-shaped pile of rock lay the Aegean Sea, and the Port of Neapolis was only a two-hours' ride away.

Philippi was a small but beautiful city. The early morning sun lit the white buildings and the colonnades that fronted the rows of shops. The street, paved with large flat stones, dropped away in front of Lydia's feet to the square which comprised the market place, forum and library, and beyond them the wide road curved toward the sea. Behind her, the same road eventually found its way to Rome, so that in a sense she stood at the crossroads of her world.

She stood at the crossroads of her life, too, she thought, and the enormity of her proposed action jerked her heart until it threatened to stop her breath. In spite of the promise of the stars which her son Ditus had pointed out to her, she was more frightened than she had ever been.

"I'd rather wait another week," she had said last night. "I'm just not ready yet."

"But the stars are ready," Ditus had insisted. He pointed at the astrology chart in front of him, its bright colors mellowed by the light from the small oil lamp. "See—Venus is ascendant, and it won't be again for a month. Venus is favorable to women. You know that."

Lydia twisted impatiently in her seat. "I don't want to be controlled by the stars."

"Mother!" Irritation roughened the smooth voice of the boy facing her. "If you insist on doing what you're doing, you need all the help you can find—not only good bankers and eager buyers, but also the favor of the gods. And the stars."

She looked at him accusingly. "You don't really believe in any of them," she said.

"Do you?" he asked.

When she hesitated, caught by his words, he shrugged. "Why take chances? You never know."

"Your father would have known," she said, but so softly he barely heard it.

"My father is dead," Ditus said harshly. "You have to accept that, Mother. You can't go on wishing he were here, wishing you still had him to lean on. You might as well wish Claudius were not the emperor of Rome."

Lydia's lips trembled slightly. Ditus was too young for compassion, she knew, but surely his own grief should have gentled him.

"Oh, by all the gods, don't cry," Ditus protested in alarm. "If you think you're strong enough to run a business by yourself, you're surely strong enough not to cry."

She was suddenly tired of being lectured by a child. Ditus

might be sixteen and almost a man in the eyes of the world, but to her he was still a child and lately, it seemed, an insolent one.

"What do you know about strength?" Lydia snapped. "What do you know about anything except games and studies? You've been away at school for half your life, and you're supposed to be here to help me, not make things worse."

He flushed with either shame or anger. "I'm sorry," he said stiffly. "I didn't mean to offend you."

"Oh, Ditus." Lydia's tears overflowed, and she stretched her hand toward him. "Let's not quarrel. I have all I can bear without having your anger on top of it."

He patted her hand with a quick gesture but did not let his fingers linger on hers. "It's just that I think I'm old enough to take over the business," he muttered, as he had said a dozen times to her since Aurelius' sudden death. "I'm not a child."

"You're barely sixteen," she said, wiping her tears. "You've had only a boy's education —philosophy, painting, a bit of mathematics. How could you possibly manage a business as complex as ours?"

"How can you?" he asked, still prickling with defiance.

"Epaphroditus!" she said sharply, using his full name as she did only when she was very angry. "How dare you? I worked beside your father for years!"

"Not at the shop," he insisted.

"Maybe not. But here at home and in the storeroom. He abided completely by my judgment about the fabric and the quality of dye. I helped with every order. I went with him to meet every ship that came into Neapolis with fabric. I know who the customers are."

"But you didn't deal with the people," Ditus insisted. "You're more of a child than I am where people are concerned. Anyone can talk you into anything."

"That's not true!" She got up and moved around the room

with agitation. "I was better than your father about setting high prices and insisting that we get them."

"But behind the scenes," Ditus persisted. "It will be different in the shop. How do you know the people won't cheat you and lie to you just because you're a woman?"

"I may be a woman," Lydia said hotly, "but I'm no fool and I must insist that you start to treat me with more respect. I am, after all, your mother."

She and Ditus glared at each other, and she felt astonished as always that, although she was tall for a woman, her son was even taller. His eyes, angry and defiant, were as dark as her own and fringed with the same long lashes. She had always been glad that the boy's hair and skin were fair like his father's. But she did not allow her approval of her son's looks to soften her expression, and it was his eyes that finally dropped.

"I'm sorry," he muttered for the second time.

Lydia turned her back and continued to move restlessly through the atrium. It was a lovely room. The walls were white with arched doorways and graceful columns. The wedding couch which had stood by the inner wall since the night Aurelius had carried her to it seventeen years before, was carved of lignum vitae and cushioned in peacock blue and deep crimson. But it was the floor which caught the visitor's attention. In the center, close to the marbled pool that caught the rain water from an opening in the roof, was an exquisite mosiac made of small black, red and white tesserae. The scene was a square, fortified tower with arched gateways and a machicolated wall. Aurelius had brought in artisans to fashion this colorful mosaic of Philippi, the city which Lydia thought even more beautiful than her native Thyatira. Lydia was careful not to step on the scene as she paced back and forth. It would be bad luck if she did.

Ditus' voice came humbly. "I really *am* sorry, Mother."

Lydia moved quickly to his side. "It's all right," she

assured him. She smoothed a hand over his hair, which was cropped short in the Roman fashion, even though she knew he didn't like to be touched. "You're sure that I can't wait a month? Or even a week? I'm so tired."

His voice was again edged with impatience. "I told you that I checked it all very carefully. Tomorrow is the day when fate will be kind to you."

"I wish I could make my own decisions without considering fate," she said rebelliously.

Ditus' tone of rebellion matched hers. "I just wish I could make *my* own decisions," he muttered.

"You will," Lydia promised. "You have your whole life ahead of you. I've told you that you don't have to go to school, that you can begin to serve as an apprentice at the shop. Can't you be patient?"

"I'll try," he said, suddenly submissive.

It was all she could do to keep from kissing his cheek. He looked very much like his father at that moment. And so, in spite of the sharp words, they had retired in peace.

Now Lydia stood in the shade of the tree and looked at the little city sparkling in the crystal morning light. She could see, if she craned her neck a little, the edge of the Roman garrison at the foot of the hill, and the sight of it brought many customers to mind. Old generals and centurions, who had moved at retirement to the sunshine and charm of Philippi, were allowed to wear the stripe of royal purple around the hem of their togas. They formed the core of Aurelius' business, only Aurelius would not be dealing with them anymore. The purple of royalty and wealth and fame would now be sold by Aurelius' widow.

I can't do it, Lydia thought with sudden bleakness, leaning against the acacia tree for support. Ditus is right. I'm only a woman. I don't know how to handle people, and I don't have anyone to help me. All the stars can do, she thought with bitterness, is push people around. One must entertain when the stars are auspicious, buy when certain stars are in the ascendancy, sell when others are on the wane. One is imprisoned, Lydia thought, by forces one can't even trust.

One thing Ditus and Lydia had never discussed: Aurelius had died on a day when his star was ascending. He should have come home flushed with success, laughing and relaxed. Instead, there had been a boy from the shop, shaking and gray, begging her to come quickly — something was wrong. Something was terribly wrong.

How could it have happened like that? How could a man like Aurelius, strong, vital, loving, just fall over like that? It wasn't fair! Life was bitter and meaningless and cruel. But before the tears could start again, Lydia beckoned her slave to follow and forced herself to step out into the sun, which fell with a sort of mercy on her chilled arms. She wished that some of the warmth could filter into her heart, but she couldn't imagine ever feeling differently than she did at this moment—lonely, frightened, bereft.

Lydia was not really conscious of walking to the shop until she stepped into the stoa, which was a sort of portico, walled at the back and open at the front to the colonnade that went around the edge of the market square. The shop and storeroom were behind a protective wall, but Aurelius had met most of his customers in the stoa where he had placed a small table and several stools, and where sunshine made a carpet of gold on the floor. It is here, Lydia thought, that I will have to act as Aurelius acted — poised and kind and able to talk to all kinds of people, to royalty and slaves, to soldiers and civilians, to Romans, Greeks, and Jews.

"Mistress Lydia!" Reuben's voice was shocked and yet warm with welcome. "I didn't expect you. That is, not so soon —" The old man's voice trailed off and he hurried to lead Lydia to one of the stools.

"Here," he begged, "sit here. The room will seem dim, coming in out of the sun. What can I do for you?"

If Reuben weren't so old, Lydia thought regretfully, she wouldn't even need to be here. He had worked with Aurelius for more than twenty years, and he knew the business better than anyone. But he had been middle aged or more when he first came to the shop, and now he was becoming forgetful and crotchety. Aurelius had said a dozen times that the old man was no longer able to deal with customers as he used to.

"I've come to work," Lydia said simply. "Someone has to run the business." She sat on the edge of a stool and wished the shop contained a cathedra chair with its comfortable sloping back. Well, she'd have one brought from home. It would, after all, be her shop now.

"But, Mistress Lydia." Reuben's voice was anxious and his hands were trembling as they worked at each other. "It's so soon. Surely you're too tired, too upset to bother with anything as difficult as the business."

The kindness in his face and voice were somehow harder to bear than Ditus' lack of sympathy. There was nothing Lydia longed to do as much as to bury her face against the old man's chest and let her tears flow.

"Just because I'm tired and sad," Lydia said, and marveled that her voice could be so steady, "doesn't mean that I'm helpless. And surely I can count on you, Reuben? Besides, Aurelius always said I would have made an excellent seller of purple if I had only been a man. Well, now —" She couldn't trust her voice, so she just shook her head and tried to smile.

"I'm not much good any more," Reuben said humbly. "I'm past the age of usefulness. I think Aurelius was planning to let me retire."

"And so you shall!" Lydia cried, trying to make her words cheerful. "You've earned your retirement. With a nice little gift of money so you can sit in the sun and have a much-deserved rest. But not just yet, my old friend. If you could give me a few months —just a few."

"I would give you years," he declared passionately. "Out of respect and love for both Aurelius and you." His mouth quivered and his eyes filled.

Old age doesn't find grief embarrassing, Lydia thought with gratitude, and reached up to press the shaking hands. "Thank you," she managed to whisper, and then they were both busy, wiping their eyes and trying to push their sorrow aside.

"Ditus will be down later," Lydia said at last. "Someday the shop will be his, but he must learn from the bottom. He must learn about fabric and the way to determine if the purple is the true dye made from shells or only the false dye made from roots. He must learn how to care for the fabric, how to handle it, how to order and cut. He's sure he can do it all now," she confided, "but he's very young. Do you think Marin will continue to work? Will he take my son as an apprentice?"

"Marin is a slave," Reuben answered with scorn. "It's not for him to say whether or not he'll teach the young master."

"Slaves have been known to run away," Lydia said slowly. "It might be hard to work for a woman, and to have an arrogant young boy as an assistant."

Reuben laughed, but his laughter had a sour sound. "It *will* be hard," he acknowledged. "But we'll manage, Lydia. Between us, we'll manage. Marin will do as I say."

Neither of them noticed that he had dropped the term "Mistress," it seemed so natural to their new situation. For the next few months, he would probably be more a father to Lydia than an employee.

Reuben left to mix wine with the warm water that was always on the small brazier in the storeroom. It is odd, Lydia thought, that I really know very little about him. Aurelius had said that he came from Jerusalem when he was a young man, not an exile exactly, but one who found it expedient to leave his own land. He was a Jew, and Aurelius said he had some peculiar ideas and refused to work on the last day of the week. But he worked so hard on the other six that Aurelius never complained. Besides, there were always Roman and Greek holy days that had to be considered, and even Aurelius, who claimed no religion at all, was glad to acknowledge other men's sacred days.

"It gives us more time to be together," he used to say to Lydia.

But I mustn't allow myself to dwell on that, she thought firmly, I must start to think about the business.

Reuben came back with a cup of warm, diluted wine in his hands.

"Drink this," he urged. "It will make you feel better, and then, if you wish, we can get to work."

2

A shadow fell across the floor, and Lydia looked up from her books to see Valleius Tatinius standing in the doorway.

"Mistress Lydia," he said with civility, bowing his head with the abrupt Roman gesture of greeting.

"Valleius Tatinius," she said formally, but her smile was warm. "Won't you come in? It's been a long time since you've been to our shop. I don't believe I've seen you since my husband died."

It is astonishing, she thought to herself, how easily she could say those words now. Reuben had been right when he told her that time and work would bring a form of healing to her. If at night she still wept into her pillow, at least she was able to put on a brave and smiling face for those who came to buy.

Valleius looked rueful. "I've been hesitant to come. I was fond of your husband, and I didn't know —well, how the business would be with him gone."

"How well a woman could handle things?" Lydia suggested, and her smile was rueful, too.

"It's not a usual situation," Valleius admitted. "But I have ordered some new wool for togas, and I need some purple. Do you have anything of value?"

"I think so," Lydia said. "Or at least, it appears to be cloth worthy of such an honor."

23

There was no flippancy in her tone. She knew with what pride the stripe of royal was worn. It was a visible symbol of courage and of devotion to Rome.

"Here," she went on, "let's go into the storeroom. I have several samples, newly arrived from Thyatira, to show you."

But instead of following her immediately, the tall Roman hesitated. "Do you mind if my slave and my seeress step in out of the sun?" he asked. "She's been prophesying all morning and she's hot and very agitated. If they could sit in the shade here on the floor?"

"By all means," Lydia responded. "Bring them in and welcome."

Valleius put his head outside the stoa and spoke sharply. Immediately, a tall black slave, dressed in a short tunic, came in, pulling a slight, cringing girl behind him.

"She's chained," Lydia said in shocked tones. "Surely you shouldn't keep her chained."

"She's totally mad," Valleius explained. "Most of the time it's safe to leave her unbound, but today has been a trying one. She's restless and might hurt herself."

The girl's eyes darted around the shop with terror. "There is death here," she proclaimed in a high voice.

The tall slave clapped a firm but gentle hand over her mouth. "Be quiet," he said. "This isn't the place for you to speak. Just sit down and try to cool off." He raised his black eyes to Lydia. "Forgive us, mistress. She's overwrought."

The girl's hands twisted and strained, and Lydia could see that the chains bit into the young flesh.

"May I offer her a drink of cool water?" Lydia asked Valleius. "She seems so agitated, and the chains are heavy."

"Thank you," the Roman said. "Keep her quiet, Nuba. I'm tired of the sound of her voice."

Lydia looked at the slave with such apprehension that

Valleius laughed. "Don't worry, Mistress Lydia. Nuba would never be other than kind to her. She's worth a hundred times more than he is, and he knows what would happen to him if anything hurt her."

Lydia went back into the storeroom where Ditus was working at the cutting table, his bent head dusky gold in the light from the opening onto the courtyard. Neither slave was in evidence, so Lydia asked Ditus if he would fetch water for the girl.

"I'm not a slave," he muttered but went to get the cup.

Lydia returned to the stoa. "My son will bring the water," she said. "Now, sir, if I might show you the cloth?"

Valleius followed her into the storeroom. In a few minutes they were so deep in conference over the shade and texture of materials that Lydia was unaware that Ditus had stayed in the stoa. As she searched for another sample, she found he was not at his worktable.

"Ditus!" she called. "Where are you?"

The boy came slowly into the room. "Yes?" he asked, but the tone was inattentive.

"Will you get the Magistrate some of that new purple wool? The kind that is woven in stripes. It's somewhere in the back. Reuben will know."

The boy seemed to come suddenly awake. "*I* know where it is," he said, and his voice was cold.

"Your son is not fond of female authority," Valleius said with amusement. "It's painful for him, isn't it?"

Lydia shrugged. "He's too young to take over the business. And my daughter is younger still. For several years —for as long as necessary —he will have to bow to my authority, however humiliating that might be to him."

"It's as hard to grow up as it is to fight a battle," Valleius said. "It's too bad the boy won't have a man to help him."

"It's something I have to deal with," Lydia said, a little sharply.

"Of course. Forgive me for being personal."

Lydia tried to smile. "It is I who should apologize. I was meddling when I suggested that the girl should not be chained."

"Erosa?" Valleius' voice sounded surprised, as though he had forgotten the conversation in the stoa. "She's a fantastic source of income to me. You needn't worry about her. Nuba guards her with his life. No man will ever touch her. She may be wholly mad at times, but she sees into the future. Really she does. And people are willing to pay dearly for the knowledge of what will happen to them."

"She's beautiful!" The young, hot voice of Ditus caught Lydia and Valleius completely by surprise. They had not heard him come back, and they stared at him in astonishment.

He threw the roll of cloth on the table roughly. "Doesn't it seem strange to you, sir, that she should be both mad and beautiful? As though a mistake had been made?"

Valleius' brows raised. "Those are deep questions to come from one so young. Have you a budding philosopher on your hands, Mistress Lydia? As well as an appreciator of beauty?"

Lydia saw the color climb into Ditus' face and she spoke in quick defense. "He's been educated in philosophy. It's natural that it should spill over into his thinking. As for beauty, one need not be educated to appreciate it."

"Especially," said Valleius with a smile, "if he has been exposed to it since his cradle." He was looking at Lydia directly, so she could not mistake his meaning.

Lydia felt heat in her own cheeks, but she kept her eyes steady. "Thank you," she said. "Though Ditus might find it hard to believe that the same word could be used to describe that tormented young girl and his weary old mother."

"Don't be foolish," Valleius said crisply. "You aren't old, and if I judge correctly, you aren't weary either. You enjoy being the head of this shop. Don't look to her leaving soon, my young friend," he added to the scowling Ditus. "She thrives on this. Comfort yourself with your philosophical thoughts."

Abruptly, he was all business. "I like this," he barked, pointing at the roll on the table. "Cut off enough for two togas. No, three. Who knows when you'll have something again of such obvious value. How much?"

Lydia indicated with a gesture that Ditus was to measure and cut the purple, then she followed Valleius into the stoa for the final reckoning. The bargaining was done without personal comments, and when it was finished, Valleius sat back on his stool and smiled.

"You drive a hard bargain," he said.

Lydia kept her voice cool and prim. "I charge what the cloth is worth."

Valleius was silent for a moment and then he said without preface, "My wife has been talking about you. She'd like to meet you."

"I think we've already met," Lydia demurred. "At the library once when I went for a dramatic reading. She was there with a mutual friend."

"I mean socially. She thinks you must be a woman of great talent and courage. Would you join us for dinner some day?"

"I'd love to," Lydia said warmly. "Since my husband died, I've been committed to the work here and to my children. It would be pleasant to dine with you and your wife."

Valleius' face showed pleasure. "Shall we say two days from now? We'll eat well before sundown. Would you like me to send Nuba for you, or do you prefer to bring your own slaves?"

"I have my own slaves," Lydia said. "Or, if he's not busy, Ditus might even bring me and then come after me."

"He'd be welcome to stay."

"And be bored with the conversation of the elderly?" Lydia's voice was light. She had caught a glimpse of her son moving just beyond the door and knew he was listening. "No, thank you very much, but it will be better if I come alone. Will you express my gratitude to your wife?"

Valleius rose. "We're the ones who will be grateful for your company. Come, Nuba, wake the little one and let's go."

The little diviner had fallen asleep on the floor. Her face had lost its tormented look, and her dark lashes lay curved against her smooth olive skin. Her hair curled in tight ringlets like a cap. When she was quiet like this, she was as beautiful as Ditus had claimed.

The black slave stooped without a word and gathered the slight body into his arms. He carried her with a curious impersonal touch as though she were a bolt of cloth —but a treasured bolt, Lydia saw, and one that must be protected against damage. The girl looked like a young child, but Lydia knew she was not a child. Under the cream-colored tunic was the figure of a woman.

"Perhaps she'll be awake and alert the night you come," Valleius said, glancing casually at his slave. "If so, I'll have her tell your future. Would you like that?"

Lydia laughed. "It would be nice to know if the year will end with a profit on the records."

"Until you grace our house, then," Valleius said, and bowed crisply. He turned and strode toward the street, followed by the tall slave carrying the sleeping girl.

"I hope you won't have any faith in what she says."

Lydia turned with surprise at the gruff sound of Reuben's voice. Every week she had promised herself that she would let him retire, but every week there was another need for his help. It was true, as Aurelius had said, that the old man was crotchety and sometimes forgetful, but he was clever and knowledgeable and Lydia felt oddly attracted to him.

"And I hope you will," Ditus said hotly. It was obvious that both had been listening and that both were interested in Valleius' offer of a fortune-telling.

"The Lord God finds such false prophecies an abomination," Reuben said somberly. As he aged, there seemed to be a breaking down of the reserve that had kept him such a private person for so long. Or perhaps it was something about Lydia's affection for him that encouraged him. This was the second time in as many days that he had referred to his God.

"Rubbish!" Ditus sputtered rudely.

"Apologize at once," Lydia snapped. "You're not to talk to older people like that. You know better."

To her surprise, it was Reuben who spoke up. "He's a man, at least in years. He has a right to his own opinion."

"I don't understand either of you," Lydia said helplessly. "You come at me from opposite sides but you won't allow me to smooth things out."

"A young man must honor his parents," Reuben said. "But I'm not his father. He needn't agree with me."

"Agree, no," Lydia concurred. "But he must respect you. That's only right."

Reuben peered at the boy and smiled. "So—are you planning to say you're sorry?"

Ditus grinned at the old man. "You're a sly one, Reuben. You know how to slide around anyone. Is it your god who gives you such clever ways?"

There was mockery in the young voice, but Reuben ignored it. "You're too ignorant to know what my God will or won't do. I wouldn't waste the words on you. It would be like throwing pearls before swine. But you, Mistress Lydia." He turned toward her and his eyes were burning. "When you're tired of foolish things like the whims of the stars or the mad rantings of soothsayers, then come to me and ask about the Lord God, Jehovah, holy be his name."

There was a strange little kick over Lydia's breast bone, and she felt a little frightened. She couldn't take her eyes away from Reuben's, and she could not think of a suitable reply.

It was Reuben who turned away. "Well, let it be," he muttered. "The time's not yet. You're not ready for the truth. When the time comes, I'll know."

"Listen, Mother," Ditus said, catching at her arm and pulling her toward him. "Reuben's god isn't any different from any other gods. But that girl—that girl of Valleius'. There's something about her. She looked at me today, and it was like looking into the center of the sun. You listen to her. We could use some prophecy in our lives."

Reuben only snorted and moved into the storeroom, but Lydia stood looking at her son for a long minute.

"You really *do* believe," she said softly.

"Believe what?" he asked in scorn, but his young voice cracked. "I just think there's something about that girl. That's all."

"We'll see," she murmured. "Go on with the cutting of that purple and then—we'll see."

3

Lydia's dressing room was on the shaded side of the house, so the first cool breeze of early evening had begun to blow through her open window as she prepared herself for Valleius' dinner. She sat before a metal mirror while a slave curled her hair and piled it high like a dark, shining crown.

In the mirror Lydia saw her daughter, Minta, come into the room and perch on the side of the bed. Minta drew her knees up under her chin and wrapped her arms around her legs. She was at the awkward age, self-conscious and despairing of her undeveloped womanhood. Now she mourned, "I'll never be as beautiful as you."

"Nonsense!" Lydia said firmly. "You're already a lovely girl. And besides, you shouldn't tell your mother she's beautiful. It might go to her head!"

"Well, it's true," the girl repeated, her voice a little shy. "Father must have told you so all the time."

Lydia kept her voice steady with an effort. "Your father was very kind. Here, Kora, get that strand of hair. It's slipping."

"So there's no one to tell you now," Minta explained. "You must miss it. I'd want people to tell me if I were pretty."

Lydia swung around to face her daughter. "You are, Minta. You're as pretty as any thirteen-year-old girl can be.

In another year or so, you'll be rounder and less awkward. I remember when I was thirteen. I was nothing but angles and bones."

"Truly, Mother?"

Lydia smiled. "Yes, truly."

"Ditus is always telling me I'm ugly. Like a picked chicken, he says."

"Ditus needs lessons in diplomacy and kindness," Lydia retorted. "But life is difficult for him just now, Minta. You'll have to be patient with him."

"Why is it so difficult for him? He doesn't have to go to school, and since he thinks he knows so much about the business, he ought to be pleased with himself to be able to work there."

"But only as an apprentice," Lydia reminded her. "And with his mother as his employer. It's hard for a young man."

"Young man!" Minta's voice was scornful. "He's only two-and-a-half years older than I am."

"Wait another two-and-a-half years," Lydia said. "You'll be surprised at how old you'll feel."

She turned toward her mirror again and watched critically as Kora placed a slender gold pin against her piled hair. She would have preferred the silver pin with the stole she was wearing, but the silver only accented the hint of gray in her hair. She wanted to feel young tonight. Young and carefree. She didn't want to think about being a widow or a businesswoman or a mother.

"Why are you going out?" Minta's voice slid into sulkiness. "You're gone most of every day. You ought to stay home in the evenings."

Lydia had been expecting this ever since she had announced her intention of spending an evening at the home of Valleius Tatinius. So, she had an answer ready. "I'm not away from *you*," she argued. "You're in school all day. I'm usually home before you are. And you won't be alone this evening. You and Sidri always spend your evenings in your room giggling. You hardly ever seek out my company."

"Sidri's only a slave," Minta protested.

Lydia spoke sharply. "Don't be ridiculous. You've never said that about Sidri in your entire life, and she's been with us since you were both babies."

"Well, she *is* only a slave," Minta insisted.

Lydia stood up and her voice was cool. "Well, if she doesn't suit you, perhaps we should sell her and look around for someone else."

Minta's eyes stretched wide with astonishment. "Mother!"

Lydia smiled. "See. I knew you didn't mean what you were saying. Now, stop being foolish about my being away for one evening. I need a little time to laugh and relax. I thought *you* would understand that."

Minta looked ashamed. "I do, Mother. I really do. I was just feeling jealous. I wish I could go out and stay half the night, the way Ditus does. Just once," she amended hastily, seeing her mother's expression.

But Lydia's astonishment was not at Minta's innocent and rebellious wish. She dismissed Kora with a nod and then chose her words carefully. "I wasn't aware that Ditus —that he stayed out half the night, as you put it."

Too late Minta realized her indiscretion, and a guilty red climbed into her cheeks. "Oh, not half the night," she said breathlessly. "You know how I exaggerate. But —but he is free to go —places."

"Ditus is a boy. And sixteen," Lydia explained. "You're not nearly so old, and a girl at that." She tried to make her voice very casual. "What does he do, do you know?"

But Minta was being careful of her words. "I don't know; he wouldn't take *me* into his confidence."

Lydia looked at her daughter closely. The children had always covered up for each other, from the time they were

tiny, and it had never been any use trying to force an inter-
rogation. Having slipped into indiscretion once, Minta
would be doubly careful.

"Well, I'm sure it's nothing to worry about," Lydia said,
making the words as light as possible. "There! Do I look all
right?"

"You're perfect," Minta said, her voice young and serious. "How do you get your hair to stay like that? Mine
never will."

"You have your father's hair," Lydia comforted. "Thick
and shining and straight. The style won't always be these
ridiculous ringlets piled up like this. Some day, you'll have
the perfect hair for a new, simpler style, and then *I* will look
ridiculous."

Minta's dimple flashed, and she reached over to smooth
the heavy drapery of her mother's ivory-colored stola.
"There! Will Ditus take you?"

"No, one of the slaves will escort me. But Ditus may
come for me later. Perhaps you'd remind him when the
water clock shows that it's time."

"If Ditus is around, I'll send him," Minta promised.

Lydia decided to ignore the idea that Ditus might not be
around. The slave who escorted her could very well bring
her home. There was no point in making an issue of Ditus'
apparent irresponsibility, especially to his younger sister.
But Minta's revelation of Ditus' absence at night was something that needed checking into. If only Aurelius' calm
judgment and steady sense of right and wrong were still
available to her. She had begun to believe that the loneliness of widowhood was not as dreadful as the *aloneness*.
Aurelius' touch was something she wanted, but Aurelius'
wisdom was something she *needed*. And if Aurelius could
never give her stability or perspicacity again, she would
have to find someone or something to give her the strength
and wisdom she needed.

The Tatinius home was large, and, like Lydia's, built in the Roman fashion. The atrium opened to a sort of office and then into the peristyle with its lovely formal garden effect. Valleius met her at the door and took her to meet his wife.

Fulvia Tatinius was a tall, graceful woman with dark hair piled in the same style as Lydia's. Her carefully draped stola was trimmed in deep crimson. Her smile was warm and friendly, but her eyes were cautious.

"I have longed to renew our acquaintance," she said in a slow, husky voice. "I was interested in your views that day at the library, and I am fascinated with the idea of a woman having the courage to take over her husband's business."

Before Lydia could respond, Valleius' light laughter was heard. "Fulvia is convinced that women are superior to men in every area of life. She finds running a household only child's play; I think she would like to lead armies or design aqueducts."

Was there a current of irritation under the teasing sound of the words? Lydia wondered. But when she looked at her host, his eyes were crinkled with laughter.

His wife made a mock gesture of reprimand and then smiled at her guest. "Men pretend to think women are helpless, only because it feeds their vanity. In truth, they share our opinion that we're superior, and it frightens them."

"Oh, surely not," Lydia protested, smiling. "Aurelius, my husband, carefully reinforced my father's teaching that women are supposed to be clever only if they can do it charmingly."

Fulvia's eyes warmed. "And do you do it charmingly?" she asked.

"Do what?"

"Be clever enough to run a business without making men so jealous that they refuse to buy from you?"

Lydia spoke in a sober voice. "I need business from men. It would be foolish of me to antagonize them —in whatever way. I couldn't manage the business, anyhow, without having been carefully initiated into its complexities by my husband while he lived, and without the good and faithful service of Reuben, an elderly man who worked for Aurelius for years. So you see I depend on men."

"A shrewd old man, Reuben is," Valleius interposed. "But you would be wise if you never brought about a conflict of loyalty between his God and yourself. He's a fanatic," he finished flatly.

"Not really a fanatic," Lydia demurred. "A man with convictions, certainly, but is that so wrong?"

"Come," Fulvia begged. "We're standing here as though we had no place to sit. Come and sit on the couches over here. We aren't having any other guests, Mistress Lydia. We thought we would just enjoy you."

Lydia sat on the indicated couch and looked at her hostess. "There's nothing so awkward as a woman alone," she commiserated. "If my husband were living, the men could dine together and we women could eat and talk together."

"Not in my house," Fulvia said decidedly, and Lydia saw the amusement in Valleius' eyes. "Sometimes, of course, we have only men as guests, and then I retire as I should. But we tend to mix our guests —men and women together. We're not old-fashioned in that respect."

"Old-fashioned is another word for conventional," Valleius said. "I thank the gods that my wife is daring and not concerned about what people think."

"The gods!" Fulvia said. "What do you care about what the gods think? You're a pagan and proud of it."

"Not a pagan," her husband protested with good humor. "Romans are willing to acknowledge the existence of many gods, of all gods. But most of us are unwilling to commit ourselves deeply. And some of the practices of

worship seem more like entertainment to me than reverence."

"The worship of Dionysius?" Lydia asked lightly, sure
that she would not be offending her host. His background
would not allow him to look kindly on the orgies of Greek
worship. Some Romans would, but not this man who must
think as Aurelius had about the blood-letting and prostitu-
tion.

Valleius snorted with laughter. "My wife would never
permit me to even visit such an affair," he said.

"Permit?" Fulvia's voice was high with incredulity.

"Truly," Valleius insisted. "Mistress Lydia, weren't there
things you permitted your husband to do? Or didn't permit, as the case may be."

Lydia laughed. "I'm sure Aurelius would have said so,"
she admitted. "I always thought of myself as an obedient
wife."

To talk of Aurelius so lightly was a stab of pain in her, yet
at the same time, there was a curious release in speaking of
him without the studied formality required of grief.

"Aurelius was a great man," Valleius said quietly. "I
knew him well. Come, my dear, surely dinner is ready to be
served," he added abruptly to his wife.

"Of course," Fulvia said. "Come, Mistress Lydia, our
dining room is this way."

The meal was delicious, served on a low table with wide
couches flanking it on three sides. Since there were only
three diners, each reclined on a couch alone. Lydia was
charmed by the fact that her host seemed perfectly contented to eat with only two women reclining at his table.
His attitude was tinged with mockery at times, with con-
descension at others, but for the most part, he seemed to
find the conversation stimulating and pleasant. Lydia discovered that she was enjoying herself more than she had
since Aurelius died. She hadn't realized how much she

missed the sparring and sparkle of adult dinner conversation until now.

When the meal was finished and the slaves had put the sandals back on their mistress' feet, Lydia and Fulvia walked together back to the large salon. Valleius, with a brief word of apology, had gone toward the rear of the house.

Fulvia laughed indulgently. "He's checking his precious Erosa," she explained. "He wants her to prophesy for you, but of course, if she's too agitated she doesn't do well. I think he wants to impress you."

"Impress *me*?" Lydia laughed lightly. "I find that incredible."

"My husband admires courage," Fulvia said. "And he needs a seller of purple in this town. He would hate it if he had to go even as far as Neapolis for the bands to trim his togas. So would the others who are permitted to wear them. You're necessary to the Roman garrison, you know."

"And they're as necessary to me," Lydia admitted. "My business would suffer drastically without them."

Fulvia shrugged. "Then you probably want to impress each other. It's natural. And Erosa is his most prized possession."

"After his family, I'm sure," Lydia protested.

"I give him only pleasure," Fulvia said without emotion. "Erosa brings both money and prestige to him. Who else owns a slave who can accurately foresee the future? She's no fake, Mistress Lydia. I hope she will say only good things for you."

Lydia made a motion of protest and Fulvia apparently misunderstood.

"If she's able to prophesy, it will be Valleius' delight and privilege to let her see your future. Please don't insult him by offering to pay."

"It isn't that," Lydia said slowly. "Reuben—the old man in our shop—he told me it was wrong to listen to her. He was so intense about it that I can't help feeling a bit uneasy."

Fulvia's eyes showed interest. "What do you mean — wrong?"

Lydia shook her head. "I'm not sure. His God would — what did he say —oh, yes, he said it would be an abomination to his God."

Fulvia didn't laugh. "There would be a certain satisfaction in having a God who said what was right and what was wrong, wouldn't there? If I were going to embrace a religion, it would have to have a God like that. One who said, 'Yes, you may' and 'No, you may not' and then never changed —as the stars do."

Lydia stared at her hostess without speaking. Wasn't that exactly what she had been feeling earlier in the evening? Hadn't she, too, been feeling the need for someone or something to give her rules for living? But it hadn't occurred to her that it might be a god. She had thought only of Aurelius who had known so surely what to do.

Valleius came into the room, and behind him the tall, black slave was leading Erosa. Tonight there was no frenzy or agitation in the girl. Her face was quiet, and her eyes seemed half-drowned in sleep.

Valleius' voice was hearty and pleased. "Well, Mistress Lydia, we're in luck. Erosa is at her best, mild as milk and not at all sulky. Come, let her take your hand and tell you what the stars have in store for you."

The slave's sleepy eyes slid toward Lydia, and she held out her hand with a coaxing gesture.

"Mistress," she said in a purring little voice. "Shall I tell your future?"

And Lydia, with a sense of reluctance which she had not anticipated and would not have been able to explain, waited for the girl who walked toward her with her small hand outstretched.

4

Erosa's hand was cold and lifeless, like the hand of a corpse, Lydia thought with dismay. Other soothsayers had prophesied to her, but their hands had been normal and warm.

"You're afraid of me," the girl said quietly. "Master, I can't see into her future if she hides behind her fear."

"Nonsense!" Lydia interposed. "Why should I be afraid?"

She forced her hand to lie quietly in the cold fingers. This was, after all, only an entertainment, a game to be played. Why did she allow Reuben's warning to disturb her?

"If you're distressed, Mistress Lydia," Valleius said smoothly, "you needn't hear her, of course. Some people are made nervous by her uncanny sight."

Was he testing her? Lydia wondered. Was he trying to determine just how much courage she really had? And, in fact, how much did she have? To face a buying public was one thing. To face a girl who was admittedly mad and who knew the unknown was something else.

And for the latter, she realized suddenly, she didn't have Reuben at her back. She had not known how much she depended on him.

"I'm not distressed," she said calmly to her host. "Let the child say what she will."

"I'm not a child," the girl screeched with unexpected

venom. "I'm a seeress, a magician, a prophetess." She turned toward Nuba with a petulant look. "Make them honor me, Nuba."

The black face was expressionless, but his voice was silky with persuasion. "They honor you, my lady." His dark eyes slid toward Fulvia and Lydia with a quick apology for the use of the title. "Of course, they do. They hunger for your words."

"Of course," Lydia said smoothly. "Your master has promised that you will look into my future. Anyone would be eager to learn what tomorrow holds."

The mad eyes riveted themselves on Lydia's face. Slowly, the round lids lowered themselves until once more the girl's eyes acquired a sleepy, unfocused look.

"You have known great sorrow," the young voice began, rising and falling with a mesmerizing sort of cadence. "But your sorrow is not ended yet. You will know grief and much worry, and your business will be threatened by — by —"

Here the words stumbled to a halt, and there was silence in the room.

"By what?" Lydia prompted, although a gesture of her host's hand indicated that she should not interrupt.

The girl twisted her head as though she were uncomfortable. "I can't see," she whimpered. "There's something there —something blocking my sight."

"Don't you see any success for me at all? Any happiness?" Lydia persisted.

"I don't know," the little slave said, turning her head from side to side in what appeared to be pain. "I can't see. Something blocks me. Something very large, something bright. Something that hurts my eyes to look upon."

Valleius spoke abruptly to the silent Nuba. "Take her away," he said. "I thought she would be in the right mood, but it appears that she isn't."

"Come, Erosa," Nuba began, but the girl twisted herself out of his hands.

"No," she shrilled. "I *am* in the right mood. And I can see the future. For you, master, I can see exactly what will happen to you. I can." She stood before her master, her head tipped back. "I can see that something will make my lady different —something because of *her*." She made a derisive gesture toward Lydia. "And you won't be able to change it," she added sadly.

Valleius tried to silence her, and Fulvia looked uncomfortable. The girl ignored them both and turned back to Lydia.

"It's only *your* life I can't see," she cried.

Lydia's hand ached where the cold little fingers clutched it, and she tried to pull away. "I'm sorry I'm such a bad subject," she said breathlessly to Valleius. "Perhaps it's too soon since Aurelius —"

"It's not Aurelius," the girl said. "He's dead. What does he know of the things that will happen to you?"

She never knew whether the girl loosened her grip or whether her own strength suddenly increased. Lydia knew only that her hand was free and she was able to stand back from the little slave, breathing hard.

"I think your little seeress may be tired," she said to Valleius, marveling that her voice could be so matter-of-fact.

Nuba took Erosa's arm, but the girl kicked and clawed. "I want to say more to her," she cried. "I want to tell her what the old man will..."

But what the old man would do —or, for that matter, who the old man was —was never to be quite clear. The girl's voice stopped so quickly that one would have thought she was throttled. But it was no human hand that silenced her. She fell to the floor, frothing and writhing.

Nuba was calm and efficient. His dark hands held her

head steady and kept her tongue from strangling her. In a few moments, the slender body was quiet.

"I'm sorry, Master," Nuba said in his expressionless voice. "The demon that possesses her has been angered."

"It doesn't matter," Valleius said. "This hasn't been Mistress Lydia's favorite form of entertainment, anyhow. Put her to bed. See that she's warm."

"Yes, Master." And once more Lydia saw Nuba stoop and lift the slight body into his arms and carry her off as effortlessly as though she were a doll.

Valleius shrugged and looked at his guest. "I had thought she would amuse you. I'm sorry that it all turned out so badly."

"Perhaps it didn't really turn out badly," Fulvia said, her voice a little loud. "Perhaps there really *was* something about Mistress Lydia which kept the girl from seeing."

"I don't know what it would be," Lydia said soberly. "Perhaps I wasn't believing enough."

"Perhaps," Valleius said, but his attention was clearly somewhere else. "Would you both excuse me for a minute? Nuba is excellent with the girl, but sometimes —sometimes it's better if I oversee things."

"Of course," Lydia said and watched him leave the room. She turned to see Fulvia looking at her intently.

"May I speak freely?" Fulvia said and motioned to a couch where they might sit down.

"Certainly," Lydia said. "Were you troubled by what the girl said to your husband?"

Fulvia made a small grimace with her mouth. "No, not really. It's very possible that I might change, and that you might be the cause of it. Friendships change people, and I think we will be friends. And Valleius has never been able to really prevent my thoughts —nor even my actions at times. No, I wasn't troubled. I'm sure he wasn't either."

"He really believes her, though."

Fulvia nodded. "Yes, he does. So do I. That's why I wanted to ask—why did you resist her so? What do you think she was talking about when she spoke of the light?"

"I don't know," Lydia answered.

"Perhaps the gods you worship...," Fulvia ventured.

"If I had any childhood gods," Lydia answered, "my husband's practical ideas abolished my beliefs. He was a pagan, and so am I."

"What of the old man in the shop?" Fulvia asked. "What of his god?"

"What has that to do with me?"

"I don't know. I only—I wish that there were really something in the world—or in the heavens—that could strengthen us and teach us. Some fixed mark to guide us."

"Perhaps if you studied the stars?" Lydia suggested, from courtesy, not conviction.

But Fulvia shook her head with irritation. "I *have* studied them. I've read of the worship of many gods. I've been searching all my life. But the gods offer nothing. No comfort. No hope. Don't you ever feel this?"

Lydia was silent for a minute. "Yes," she admitted at last. "While Aurelius lived, it wasn't so bad. He was such a good man, such a wise one, that I didn't need any other god."

"Valleius is not that good. Or that wise," Fulvia confided. "He's greedy and, like most men, I suspect he may sometimes be unfaithful to his wife. I don't really care. But I need something—something strong and good."

Lydia sat staring at hr new friend. She had seldom met this kind of honesty and she was moved by the naked revelation.

"You shame me, Mistress Fulvia," she said at last. "I've also been disillusioned by the study of the stars, but I haven't thought of finding something to replace it. I've been very insensitive, it seems."

Fulvia smiled. "But I've had nothing else to occupy my mind during recent months. My children are all grown; the youngest has gone to Rome for military training. I have nothing to do but think, while you have had many things to fill your life."

Lydia smiled and spread her hands. But Fulvia's kindness did not really absolve her, she thought.

Fulvia twisted her head toward the distant sound of her husband returning. "If you discover anything—about the old man and his god, I mean —will you tell me?"

Lydia had only time to nod before her host came back into the room.

"The girl's quiet now," he said. "Since my first attempt at entertainment failed so dismally, what can we do to amuse you, Mistress Lydia?"

"Nothing, thank you," Lydia answered. "I really must be going. My daughter is young yet, you know, and although the slaves are quite dependable, I'm always a little uneasy away from home late in the day. Will you forgive me if I don't stay late?"

Before Valleius could answer, Fulvia spoke warmly. "We understand and would be just as uneasy under the same circumstances. But now that we've met, Mistress Lydia, really met, surely I'll see you again?"

"I very much hope so," Lydia said. "We don't work the last day of the week at our shop. It is a whim of Reuben's which we find pleasant to copy. And I'm always free in the evenings, and occasionally we're not too busy during the afternoon. I'll get word to you very soon and I hope you'll come to my house."

Valleius looked gratified. "I was right, then, in bringing you two together. I thought you would be congenial."

Lydia's slave was called and the final farewells were said. But at the door, Fulvia caught her guest's hand. "You won't forget?" she said.

"I won't forget," Lydia said gently, and their fingers clung for a minute. I've found a friend, Lydia thought gratefully, a woman whose mind will challenge and stimulate mine. It will be good to have someone to talk to again.

It was not until she reached home that she remembered that Ditus was to have come after her. There was no lamp lit in his room, and he was nowhere in the house. A quick glance into Minta's room showed her daughter curled up in her bed, sound asleep.

Or was she, Lydia wondered with sudden suspicion, seeing the lashes move against the round cheek. Lydia hesitated, questioning the wisdom of speaking to Minta. Frustration and worry seemed to sweep over her like a wave. I don't know what to do, she thought bleakly, I don't know what to do. The memory of Erosa's prediction of worry and trouble added to her unhappiness.

With a feeling of despair she turned from the small room of her daughter and went to the silence and loneliness of her own room.

5

Before she slept, Lydia heard Ditus come in and creep stealthily toward his room. She was tempted to confront him and demand an account of the evening. But she reminded herself that he was not a child and that he had been away from home and its discipline for several years. Surely there was enough of his father's fine qualities in the boy to keep his adventures innocent, and she could wait until morning to talk to him.

At breakfast, Ditus was cheerful and casual. For as long as Minta sat with them, Lydia matched her son's breezy manner. But when Minta hurried off to the classes held for daughters of the merchants and wealthier citizens of the town, Lydia decided to stop playing the role she had assumed.

"I'd better start out, too," Ditus announced. "Marin has been grouchy lately and it might be well for me to arrive before he does."

"Marin can wait," Lydia said. "I'll explain your delay." She saw the nervous jerk of the boy's shoulders and knew that he wanted to say that he didn't need a woman to make excuses for him, but she went on firmly. "I want to talk to you. About last night. And other nights, I suspect."

Ditus' eyes were wide with a look of such artless amazement that, if she hadn't known better, she would have believed the boy had been safely in his bed at sundown.

"Don't play cat and mouse with me," she said sharply. "I won't act the fool for you, Ditus. You've been going out every night, or certainly most nights, after I've gone to my room. I want to know where you've been."

His voice was sulky. "I haven't been anywhere. Just out."

"Nonsense! You don't just go out and walk the streets until half the night has gone. You must be going somewhere with someone."

He refused to meet her eyes and pressed his lips tightly together.

"Is it a girl?" she asked. "Are you seeing a girl?"

Color came into his face, but his tone of voice told her that it was anger, not shame, which brought the heat to his cheeks. "I suppose that's the only thing you can think of," he said. "It isn't young people who have lewd thoughts —it's their parents."

She felt her own cheeks flame with anger. "How dare you accuse me of lewdness?" she cried.

"You accused me first."

"I did not. I asked you a civil question."

"But with accusation in it," he retorted.

"And one you're apparently afraid to answer," she said.

This stung him. "I'm not afraid to answer," he said hotly. "And the answer is no. I have not been seeing any girls. There! Are you satisfied?"

"No, not entirely. You still haven't answered my first question. I think I have a right to know where you've been."

He took a deep breath and she could see he was trying to control his temper.

Before he could speak, she hurried to say in a voice deliberately gentled, "I'm not prying, Ditus. I want to trust you, and I apologize for blurting out the question about a girl. But we cannot live together with any degree of joy if you sneak out behind my back."

He spoke stiffly. "I wasn't aware that I was sneaking or

that I was doing anything behind your back. I didn't know that I had to report every move to you."

She continued to hold her voice down. "When you were in school, Ditus, did you go out without telling anyone where you were going?"

"No," he muttered.

"Never?"

"Maybe once —or twice."

"And when you did, did you feel you were sneaking out behind the back of authority?"

Stung again, he lowered his eyes. His mumbled reply was not clear, but she knew it had not been a denial.

"Then why do you think it's different with me?" she asked, her voice reasonable.

For a long minute, there was silence while Ditus struggled with his feelings.

"I go down to the garrison," he said abruptly.

"To the garrison?" Her voice scaled upward with amazement. "Have you ambition to be a soldier then? You're a Roman citizen —you would qualify for training if that's what you want."

"I want to be a seller of purple," he answered. "You know that."

"Then why the garrison, Ditus? And why at night?"

"Do I have your permission to be honest?"

"Certainly. Why do you think you'd have to ask that?"

"Because the truth will make you angry."

She waited, watching his face.

"I need the company of men," he said abruptly. "At school, we had all boys and men. Here at home there is only you and Minta. Everything is soft and sweet-smelling. I need rough talk and the smell of sweat."

The words were chopped short with defiance, and Lydia's instant reaction was exactly what Ditus had predicted.

"Must you be vulgar?" she asked stiffly.

"I said you'd be angry."

She turned away and struggled to compose her face as well as her thoughts.

"And do you have friends there," she said at last, "to provide the smell of sweat?"

He stiffened at her use of his own words, but he kept his voice cool. "I have friends. There are men there I admire and respect. There is one, Clement, who is my special friend."

"A boy your age?"

"No, a man my father's age. He has a son about my age who's also a friend of mine."

She stood abruptly, knowing that she was incapable of further discussion with the boy. She would have to find out who this Clement was; perhaps Valleius would know.

"We won't talk about it now," she announced. "It's time for both of us to be at the shop. But I would appreciate it in the future if you could bring yourself to share your plans with me, especially when they take you away in the evening."

Ditus' voice was as final as hers. "And I would appreciate it if you could come to trust me."

They parted, and it was the first time their anger had not been diluted with apology.

Thoroughly despondent, Lydia, accompanied by her slaves, made her way toward the shop. She was almost unaware of the bustle and beauty of the small city she loved so much. Her mind kept twisting back and forth over the conversation she had just had with Ditus. A Roman boy was taught to obey his father and to love his mother, she thought morosely, and certainly until recently, Ditus had always been an obedient and affectionate —if headstrong —boy. What was she doing wrong?

A group of men, talking loudly and laughing boisterously, came along the street and one of them jostled her shoulder.

"Your pardon," he begged, and his eyes ran appreciatively over her face. "If your husband makes you so sad, pretty one," he whispered wickedly, his black eyes twinkling, "only call on me. I could make you smile again."

Lydia's slaves drew closer to her with a protective movement, and she stared coldly into the stranger's face. This sort of thing had happened before, of course. It happened to every woman and meant nothing. But always before, Aurelius had been there to soothe her distress at the coarseness of the encounter and assure her of his protection. Now, she had no one.

Oh, Aurelius! she thought with an aching stab of loneliness and sudden tears. The grinning stranger eyed the stalwart slaves beside her with respect, shrugged, and continued on his way.

"Are you all right, my lady?" one of the slaves asked.

"Yes, I'm all right. Thank you."

But she could never really be all right without Aurelius, she thought. Never.

At the shop, she found chaos. There were several customers, all clamoring to be waited on, and Reuben was crotchety and irascible.

One of the customers was a large, heavy woman with a haughty look on her face.

"I want purple to trim the tunics of my little boys," she said imperiously. "What do you have?"

"The gentleman was here first," Reuben growled.

"Reuben, if you'll take care of the gentleman, I'll see to it that the lady is served," Lydia said, pushing away her feelings to cope with the business at hand.

The woman looked disdainfully at Lydia. "I would prefer to speak to the man who owns the shop," she announced.

For a second Lydia stood very still. She wanted to cry out, "*You* want to talk to him? Well, so do I! But he's dead — dead —" But she made herself say instead, "*I* am the owner of the shop."

"A man served me last time," the woman protested.

"That was my husband, I'm sure," Lydia agreed. "He died some months ago."

There was no expression of sympathy as the woman continued to stare at Lydia. "And you're taking his place?" she asked. "Have you no children then? Does your home manage itself without you?"

"May I show you some purple for children's tunics?" Lydia spoke rigidly, trying to ignore the anger that blazed in her. She was aware that the men in the shop were looking her way with growing uneasiness.

"All right," the woman muttered sullenly. "Something attractive, if you have it."

Lydia led her customer to the cathedra chair and after she was comfortably seated, went into the workroom. "Ditus," she said impersonally, "will you find some of the purple for children's tunics? Bring three or four rolls of the better stuff. And hurry, I have an impatient customer."

Ditus went to do her bidding. Unwilling to face the woman again without the cloth to show her, Lydia waited beside the cutting table until Ditus returned.

"Thank you," she said. "If you'll bring them, please, so the lady can see them. Maybe you'd better just stay so you can carry the rolls back. It looks as though business is going to be heavy today."

She might have been speaking to a stranger, she thought, for all the reaction he showed to her, but she couldn't take time to think of that now.

"Here you are, Madam," Lydia announced, back in the stoa. "Here are samples of some of the best purple we have for children's tunics."

The woman leaned forward and began to push through the rolls that Ditus laid in front of her.

"Do you call this purple?" the woman said scornfully,

holding up one of the brighter rolls. "It's almost crimson. Not purple at all."

"It's not customary to put the best purple on children's tunics," Lydia said, controlling her voice. "This is dyed with the false purple, of course, not with the true shellfish. But it's bright and colorful and children usually like it very much."

"I can afford the best purple," the customer announced, "and I would appreciate it if you would show it to me."

Ditus moved to get the rolls, and Lydia spoke tautly. "Will you bring some of the best, my son?"

"Your son?" The woman stared frankly from Lydia to Ditus. "Yes, I can see the resemblance to the man who served me last. How does it seem, young man, to work for a woman?"

The sheer audacity of the question caused Lydia to flush hotly. "Madam," she began, struggling for words.

Ditus interrupted smoothly. "It's always a pleasure to work with, or wait on, a beautiful woman, my lady," he said in honeyed tones that Lydia had never heard before. His eyes were brilliant under the long lashes and the woman in the chair bridled with a look of sudden satisfaction.

"I'm sure," Ditus went on smoothly, "that money is not a problem for one so obviously blessed by the gods, but may I suggest that, if it's small children you're buying for, you seriously consider these brighter hues? Children like to wear the brightest colors possible, and they don't like to be different from their playmates. At least," he said in a deprecatory way, "that was true of me when I was very small—and perhaps still is." He made a slight gesture that called the woman's attention to the bright stripe that ran the length of his tunic.

"I expect you'll be getting rid of the colored stripe soon?" she asked, her eyes devouring the boy in front of her, "so that you can wear the white tunic and toga of a man?"

"On my seventeenth birthday," Ditus admitted, "which is, uh, soon."

His seventeenth birthday is months away! Lydia thought indignantly. But there was no doubt that Ditus was handling the woman with admirable skill.

Under Ditus' wheedling voice, the choices were made at last, and the customer ignored Lydia as though she were not present. But when the time came to settle on the price, Lydia interrupted Ditus' flattering words.

"It is I who will settle the amount due, Madam," she said in a brusque voice. "Ditus, if you'll take the unwanted rolls back and cut the lengths that have been ordered?"

Reduced to errand boy again, Ditus did as he was told, but his face was sullen.

The woman bickered and quarreled over the prices, and Lydia found herself speaking more sharply than any shop owner should, especially the owner of so rich and prestigious a shop as the one where purple was sold. But at last the bargaining was completed, and the woman rose to go.

"May I say," she said at last, "that, as a devoted wife and mother, I think the place of women is in the home —where she can take care of beautiful children like that son of yours."

"Madam, what I do is hardly your business," Lydia began furiously, before she caught the stern look in Reuben's eyes. Brought to her senses by his expression, she realized she could do serious harm to the business that Aurelius had worked so hard to build, that she and the children needed if they were to continue living in their luxurious home. She swallowed her anger and forced herself to say sweetly if somewhat deceitfully, "However, I do appreciate your interest. You are kind and gracious. When my son is a little older, he will no doubt free me to go back to the business of being a woman again."

Her customer smiled in a satisfied way. "You are blessed to have so handsome a son."

There was actually a greedy look in her eyes, Lydia noted with disgust, and she could not entirely keep the edge from her words. "Thank you, Madam. I hope you will let us serve you often."

The woman's smile was stiff as she stalked from the stoa.

Relieved to be rid of her, Lydia turned back to her work only to find that Reuben was letting his own irritation show toward a customer, and for another hour the atmosphere was anything but pleasant.

Had Ditus been right? she thought with despair, as the time crawled by. Was she really incapable of dealing with people just because she was a woman? She tried to reassure herself, but she continued to be troubled and upset and wished more than once that she were safely at home instead of in the shop.

By noon the customers had disappeared. Ditus and Marin left for lunch and the usual noontime two-hour respite. Lydia and Reuben looked at each other in the sudden silence.

"I'll just stay in the shop today," Reuben offered, "so that we won't have to bother locking the shutters. You go home and rest."

"You need rest as well as I," Lydia said. "I'll send one of the slaves home for cheese and fruit and some bread. We'll just eat here where there's no one to bother us."

"If it pleases you," Reuben said agreeably. "But if you'll excuse me, I'll go into the inner room for prayer first."

Lydia was surprised. He had never done this before, but then she had never stayed at the shop during lunch hour before either. Why would a man pray in the middle of the day, and what good was prayer anyhow? She sent one of the slaves for food and then sat in the comfortable cathedra chair. But it was impossible to rest. Everything that had happened that morning ran through her mind like a ribbon looped over on itself, and the memories left a sour taste in her mouth. What was she going to do? Where could she turn? Without Aurelius, what did life hold for her?

I won't cry, she said savagely to herself. I've cried enough. But there is no comfort or strength for me anywhere. I simply don't know what to do!

Reuben was returning to the stoa, and to her surprise, all the angers and irritations that had been etched on his face were gone. They had been smoothed away as though someone had run a hand over damp clay and erased the lines.

"What have you been doing?" she asked in amazement.

"I've been praying to Jehovah, blessed be his name," Reuben said warmly. "I've been placing my burdens on him."

"Oh, Reuben," Lydia cried longingly, "I'd give anything I own if I could have a faith like that."

6

Reuben gave her a shrewd but affectionate look.

"There's no reason why you can't," he announced.

"There are a million reasons," she cried. "I wasn't brought up to know your god. I have no patience with the foolish acts of worship that I've seen in the temples of Isis or Jupiter, and I find the worship of Dionysius abhorrent. What's different about the god you pray to?"

"Why did you ask me what I'd been doing?" Reuben asked.

"Because —because you looked so different," she faltered. "All the anger and worry was gone from your face."

"Then the difference between my God and the pagan gods you've been talking about ought to be obvious. My God is able to give me peace."

"Truly, Reuben?"

"You don't know much about me, Lydia," he said slowly, sitting on one of the stools and hitching it toward her. "I've had real tragedy in my life. I lost my wife and son in childbirth, and about the same time, I got into trouble with the temple authorities, so that it seemed best for me to leave my own country. I won't go into it, but it's enough to say that if a Jew is driven from Jerusalem, the trouble is great."

"Why didn't your god protect you from the trouble? Didn't you make sacrifices?"

"You don't understand," he said, showing an unusual patience. "Some of the prophets have taught that Jehovah doesn't enjoy the smell of burning flesh. A proper sacrifice to him is a broken and contrite heart. He may have chosen not to prevent troubles from happening to me, but he kept them from destroying me."

"It would seem that a god who really amounted to anything could keep terrible things from happening to people who believed," Lydia argued.

Reuben sighed. "There's no promise in the Scripture that the Lord will make our lives a paradise. There's only a promise that he will keep us from falling into total despair. He's a God of mercy and of love, but he's also a God of justice and he makes laws we have to follow."

"Laws?"

"Yes. How do you think I survived the troubles I've just told you about? How do you think I endured losing everyone and everything I had ever loved? It was because, no matter where I went or what I did, I continued to follow the Law."

Lydia twisted in her chair. "I don't understand what you're talking about," she complained.

"Listen, Lydia, do you remember the day I said that a boy should honor his father and his mother, that day when Ditus was insolent to me?"

"Yes, of course I remember. But that's only a rule that everyone has. Everyone *knows* that a boy should be obedient."

Reuben shook his head. "I'm talking about more than a rule that people think is a good idea. I'm talking about a law from God. The Lord himself made the Law. He made it, I imagine, because early man didn't just automatically honor his parents, and so the Lord God Jehovah said, 'Honor your father and your mother that your days may be long in the land which the Lord your God gives you.'"

The lovely rhythm of the words caught at Lydia's heart. "And what all does this god expect from people?" she asked in a small voice.

"What does the Lord require of you," Reuben intoned, and it was obvious that he was quoting, "but to do justice, and to love kindness, and to walk humbly with your God."

The words faded into a vibrating silence, and Lydia felt the beauty of his statement in the very core of her being. She wanted to be still and to let the memory of what he had said pour over like a wave. But she was almost afraid of the silence.

"What's he like, this god of yours?" she asked. "What does he look like? Do you have temples like the worshipers of Isis? If you don't make sacrifices, what do you do?"

Reuben smiled. "It would take me the rest of my life to answer your questions. And even then, we wouldn't have time. You don't need all those answers anyhow. Didn't you feel a little of the wonder when I spoke the words of Scripture?"

She nodded slightly but refused to put her questions aside. "I have to know what he looks like. I wouldn't want to give him any serious consideration at all if he had two heads, or if he were half goat."

The slave came in just then, panting from his running, and began to lay out the food on a low table. There were cheeses, raised bread, olives in a small jar, and grapes, and apples.

"I'm hungry," Reuben said. "I'm sure you are, too. Shall we eat?"

"I'm too upset to be really hungry," Lydia answered. "But I suppose I ought to take something."

She put out her hand to take a slice of the cheese, but Reuben's hand covered hers. "Wait," he said. He went to the corner of the room and dipped water from a basin and let it pour over his hands, holding his fingers pointing in the air so that the water dripped from his bent wrists. Then he stepped out to the curb and rinsed his mouth and face. Coming back to the table, he stood with his head bowed and then spoke briefly in a strange, gutteral language.

"What did you say?" Lydia asked when he sat down and prepared to eat.

"I asked the Lord's blessing on this food, and on you."

Lydia took some of the food. She had thought she wasn't hungry, but the cheese was cool, the olives salty, and the bread crisp. The slave brought watered wine from the inner room, and she sipped slowly, feeling her body revive as she nourished it.

"As to what Jehovah looks like," Reuben went on as though their conversation had not been interrupted, "he's a God of spirit and of truth. He has no body. He's all powerful, all wise, merciful and good. He created the heavens and the earth."

"He's all that?" Lydia said, "and he can care for *you*?"

"It shakes the mind, doesn't it?" Reuben agreed. "I have marveled all my life, since I've been old enough to know, that God the Almighty knows and cares about his children, his chosen children," he corrected himself. "Those who were born into the Jewish nation, and those who accept him with their hearts and agree to follow the Law."

Lydia was silent, pondering the words Reuben had said. She was attracted to the whole idea, she realized, but there were too many questions filling her mind for her to be easily convinced.

Reuben spoke again. "You're having problems with Ditus. No, don't try to deny it," he said as he saw her expression. "You needn't be ashamed. If Ditus had been taught since babyhood, as I was taught, that God had *commanded* him to honor his parents, do you think he would be worrying you now?"

"Oh, I don't know," she said fretfully. "I suppose if

Aurelius and I had believed something like that, Ditus might have grown up believing."

"It's never too late to learn to believe," Reuben said. "Lydia, listen. I have a few scrolls of our Scripture, scrolls I have treasured more than life itself. Let me lend them to you so that you can read for yourself the words that come from God. Then perhaps you'll know."

"How do you know the words came from God? Couldn't they just have been written by a man?"

"When you read, you'll understand. The truth and beauty and purity of the words couldn't have come from a man's heart, although they might have been written by a man's pen. Such truth can come only from God."

Lydia simply looked into the old man's face.

"Will you read the scrolls?" Reuben asked gently. "Will you let the Lord speak to your heart?"

"I'll try," Lydia whispered.

"And in the meantime," Reuben said, "I'll pray for you, more than I've been praying. I'll ask the Lord to be a light before you, a lamp upon your way."

"Thank you," Lydia said, too tired to argue or question.

"You might try praying yourself," Reuben suggested, wiping his mouth with the linen square the slave had provided.

"When I don't believe?"

"You never know what brings the beginning of belief. It may be prayer. The Lord will hear you, even if you doubt him."

"I think," Lydia said, getting to her feet and brushing the crumbs from the folds of her stola, "I think I'm going to need more than prayer before this thing with Ditus is over. I may need a miracle."

"The Lord has worked many miracles," Reuben said. "He parted a sea, and cast a man out of a fish's belly, and he kept this Jew faithful even in a strange land where there are not even ten male Jews, which is the requirement for a minyan."

She was touched by the tone of his voice even though she hadn't the faintest idea what he was talking about.

"Then pray for a miracle for me," she said.

Reuben stood and looked at her with a solemn face. "The Lord bless you and keep you," he said in the soft, singing chant she had heard before when he seemed to be quoting. "The Lord make his face to shine upon you and be gracious to you, the Lord lift up his countenance upon you and give you peace."

She bowed her head and received the blessing with humility, and when Ditus came hurrying through the door with Marin, she was able to smile at him with the old warmth, untainted by her recent worry.

Dinner that evening was a pleasant meal. Minta was merry and talkative, and Ditus seemed to enjoy her chatter. Lydia listened to them and felt comfortable and relaxed.

Kora came to the door. "Here's a message from Mistress Fulvia," she said. "One of her slaves just brought it."

Lydia took the double tablet edged in wood with heavy wax centers. It was tied with a crimson cord and wax had been poured over the knot. Evidently the words inside were for her eyes alone.

"Is the Tatinius slave still here?" she asked.

"Yes. I think he waits for an answer."

"I'll have it ready in a few minutes," she said and pushed herself up from the couch. "Will you two excuse me? This seems to be personal."

"Maybe she's inviting you to a party," Minta said.

"Perhaps," Lydia said, making her voice casual. "When you've finished eating, Minta, find Sidri and go to your room. It will be dark before long and you'll want to get your lamp lighted while there's still plenty of time to see what you're doing."

Minta nodded, too busy stuffing cakes into her mouth to answer.

"Are you, too, going to bed, my son?" Lydia asked. "Or have you other plans?"

"I'm not sure," Ditus said and failed to meet her eyes.

Lydia only looked at the boy and then bent her head slightly and left the room. She had asked him once to share his plans; now she could only hope he would comply with her wishes. She stopped in the peristyle where the light was best and sat down on one of the marble benches to break the wax and open the cord. The words were etched on the wax inside the tablet.

"Erosa is very disturbed," she read. "She demands that Valleius bring you to our house again so she can see you. He will go to any length to keep her quiet, so I think he will be persistent about your seeing her. I don't want you to be upset, but I felt I ought to warn you about Valleius. He's very —" There were marks on the wax as though Fulvia had written a word, rubbed the wax smooth and written another, "determined. I think he'll come to see you soon."

Lydia read the message again and then used a piece of wood to smooth the wax so that Fulvia's words were gone. She hesitated briefly and then wrote with a wooden stylus, "Thank you, my friend, for writing to me. I have been wanting to talk to your husband about someone I'm curious about, so I'll look forward to his coming. And I'll heed your words."

She tied the tablets together and dropped melted wax onto the knot. Even if the slate fell into other hands, she had said nothing that would reveal Fulvia's warning.

"Warning" was a strong word, but Fulvia must have had some reason for using it, Lydia mused. She gave the slate to the waiting slave and went slowly to her room. She was very tired, but after the multitude of upsetting things that had happened during the day, she was sure she would be unable to sleep. She hadn't slept well since Aurelius' death, even before she knew Ditus was leaving the house. I'll think only about Reuben's words, she promised herself. Perhaps that will comfort me.

There was a sound at her door and she turned to see Ditus.

"I'm going out," he announced.

"Out?" she said. "It's very late, isn't it?"

Almost at once she wished she had bridled her tongue.

"You said you wanted me to share my plans with you," Ditus said in a controlled voice. "I'm trying to."

And he asked me to trust him, Lydia thought. Why is it so hard for me?

She bowed her head in a sign of acknowledgment. "Thank you, my son. May I ask —dare I ask," she went on humbly, "that you speak to me when you come back? I won't mind being wakened and it would keep me from waking later in the night and not knowing."

She could sense the struggle in his mind and knew how much he wanted to protest.

"Of course, I will," he said, his voice formal and withdrawn. "I don't want to cause you additional worry."

Don't you, she wanted to cry out. Oh, don't you, my son? Then why don't you act as I think you ought to act? Why don't you do the things I think you ought to do?

"Thank you," she said, and with great effort kept herself from adding an injunction to be careful, to come back early.

When Ditus had left the room, Lydia dismissed Kora, removed her stola and girdle, and lay on the bed in her tunic. She lay quietly for a long time, forcing her thoughts away from Ditus, making herself think instead of Reuben, remembering the peace on his face after his prayer.

If his god is real," she thought, I could learn to believe, I think, and perhaps I could endure life even without Aurelius.

"If you're real," she whispered, without any of the formalities of prayer, "show me. Make me see."

Almost immediately she fell asleep, and when Ditus stopped at her door to report that he was home, she came up out of the deepest sleep she had known since Aurelius died.

"What?" she said thickly. "Oh, Ditus, it's you. Thank you, son. Sleep well now."

He hesitated at the door, and in the dim light of the lamp he carried, his face was very young in spite of the resentful thinning of his mouth.

"Thank you," she said again, and turning over, fell deeply and peacefully asleep.

7

There was a message waiting for Lydia at the shop next morning, saying that a load of fabric had arrived from Thyatira and she could purchase new supplies at Neapolis.

This is just what I need, Lydia exulted with an unexpected rush of excitement. I'll get away from the shop, away from responsibility, away from the children. No wonder Aurelius always enjoyed this part of the work and always took me with him. It will be a little like a holiday.

In only an hour she was on her way. Accompanied by several slaves, she rode in her carriage along the wide road. It was not a smooth ride, and she could see the narrow ruts worn in the stone pavement over which the wheels of her carriage jolted. But there was no dust, and the horses traveled swiftly in the clear morning.

Mount Symbolum jutted like a cone of silver against the vivid sky, and beyond it was the Aegean. She waited for the first glimpse of the water, the vivid blue that always brought such pleasure to her.

I should have asked Fulvia to come with me, she thought suddenly. It would have been a marvelous time to get better acquainted. She could have visited the market with one of the slaves while I took care of my business at the wharf. Well, I'll surely think of it next time.

Horsemen passed them several times, cantering faster than the carriage. Lydia felt gratitude for the ordered world in which she lived. Before the Roman rule, it would have been suicidal for a woman to travel alone. But now the Pax Romana, the peace of Rome, made travel not only possible but even pleasant. It had been one of the reasons Aurelius had been so proud of being a Roman.

"The armies are harsh at times," he had said, "and not every Caesar is benevolent. But citizens are safe all over our world. Only Rome could do that."

So I can sit in my carriage and nod at soldiers who ride by, Lydia thought, and never feel my heart jerk with fear. Her thoughts had scarcely been formulated when more horses drew near, and this time they stopped. She found herself staring into the face of Valleius Tatinius.

"Oh!" Lydia gasped, and her hand flew up to cover her mouth.

"You're surprised to see me, Mistress Lydia?" His smile was gallant and his eyes were very bright.

"But of course. Are you traveling to Neapolis?"

"I am. I rode hard to catch up to you."

"How did you know I was coming this way?" Lydia asked.

"Ditus told me when I stopped at the shop. I came to talk to you."

She smiled. "That was kind of you. I told Fulvia that I hoped to get some information from you."

He swept a half bow from his saddle. "I'm at your service."

She gave a deprecatory laugh. "This isn't a good place to talk, though. You're so high and I'm so low, and the horses and wheels are so noisy that I can hardly hear you."

"I could ride with you," he said, "but I'm not sure that's such a good idea either. Why don't we go together to the inn in Neapolis? They serve passable food, and we could eat our midday meal there."

"But a woman unaccompanied," Lydia began.

"I'll come to the wharf for you so that you won't be unaccompanied. There's a private dining room where ladies are welcome. And of course we'll be coming home again long before dark."

Now, what did he mean by that last remark? Of course they'd be coming home before dark!

"So there will be no gossip," Valleius assured her. "We don't want that, do we?" and his bright eyes mocked her. Before she could answer, he had tightened his reins and kicked his horse into action. "At the ship then, in a few hours," he shouted cheerfully and flashed away from her down the road.

The man is insolent, Lydia raged to herself. Did he possibly flatter himself that she sought out his company because she was lonely?

That might be what he thinks, she conceded when the first hot anger had gone. It was possible that even Fulvia thought so. After all, Aurelius had been dead for nearly half a year, and there were those who thought a woman needed a man, any man.

But not me, Lydia thought with quick pride. After Aurelius, all men look small and insignificant. Even Valleius with all his money and all his power. What does he know of gentleness or love? Would Fulvia be the sort of person she was, evidently searching for meaning in her life, if her husband were warm and loving?

On the other hand, Lydia reflected soberly, Valleius was a strong, vital, exciting man. It was quite possible that he had turned the heads of many women. "He's very determined," Fulvia had said in her note. Was she warning Lydia of something more serious than Erosa's desire to see her?

I'm being foolish, Lydia thought. I'm reading things into a short message that were not intended. A sudden curve of the road brought her the first view of the Aegean, a shining bit of blue which looked as though a piece of sky had fallen to earth.

Lydia decided to stop tormenting herself with foolish fears and fancies and enjoy her holiday. She would recapture the mood of the morning and concentrate on her business with the owner of the merchant ship. At this moment, it was the only thing that really mattered.

The smells and noise on the wharf were almost overwhelming, and more than one head turned to stare in astonishment at the sight of a woman, accompanied only by slaves, striding toward the merchant ship. Lydia kept her head high, only pulling a fold of her pallas, her lightweight, almost sheer shawl, over the lower part of her face. It was more to keep out the odors, she assured herself, than because of modesty.

The owner of the ship was also amazed to see her, but he remembered her from the times she had come with Aurelius. After expressing his condolences over Aurelius' death, he settled down to the business at hand. Lydia's eye was sharp and she knew fabrics too well to be deceived by cheap or poorly dyed materials, and when the bargaining was finished, the owner of the ship had an expression of rueful respect on his face. If he had hoped, on seeing a woman, that he might make more than his usual profit, Lydia thought, he had been wrong. They parted with mutual expressions of courtesy, and Lydia left the ship with a feeling of pride and achievement.

Valleius was waiting for her, and she was feeling too satisfied with herself to be cool or reserved.

"My business is all finished, my friend," she said gaily, "and Aurelius would be proud of the bargaining I've done."

He fell into step beside her and his commanding presence seemed to clear a way for them through the crowds.

"You mean the ship owner was misled by your loveliness and thought he might be able to cheat you?" he teased.

She smiled, still heady with her success. "I don't know about that, but I'm certain he thought I would be as fuzzy-headed as some young girl who didn't know a distaff from a spindle. But he found out readily enough, and I got some fine purple at a decent price. The profit should be considerable."

"You ought not say such things to a customer, my dear," Valleius cautioned. "After all, I'm the one providing the profit."

"Only one of the many, sir," she corrected. "And you know you could always come to Neapolis to buy directly from the ship."

Valleius laughed comfortably and put an apparently casual hand under her elbow. "And what do I know about purple?" he said. "I always trusted Aurelius to have only the best material —just as I now trust the charming Lydia."

His fingers tightened caressingly, and Lydia felt the pressure with a prickling of her skin, a feeling of apprehension.

"Well, anyhow, the bargaining is done," she said, trying to keep her voice casual, "and now I can relax for this meal you've promised me. And then, sir," she went on in a serious tone of voice, "perhaps you'll be able to give me the information I want, and you might even be willing to advise me."

"I'm at your service," he said softly, intimately. "If I can do anything to make you happy, you know I'll do it."

This time, there was no mistaking the gentle pressure of the fingers on her arm. She smiled in reply, but the pounding of her heart jolted her into an awareness of Valleius that was as much fear as it was an acknowledgement of the man's charm.

The conversation during the early part of the meal was

casual, and it was obvious to Lydia that Valleius was putting himself out to see that she enjoyed herself. His anecdotes were amusing, and his concern for her was soothing after the months of independence. Almost without her realizing it, her defenses crumbled under his warmth and she found herself relaxed and laughing and feeling more feminine than she had felt for a long time.

Gradually, he worked his way around to the subject of Erosa, and he was so beguiling in his explanations that Lydia found herself almost wanting to do as he suggested.

"I'm not eager to hear my future," Lydia said finally. "Erosa seemed to be aware only of doom at our last meeting and to tell you the truth, I've had about all the doom I can stand lately."

"She was angry that night," Valleius conceded. "She must have felt you endangered her somehow. She'll know better next time."

"I? A danger to her? That's ridiculous."

"Not so ridiculous." His voice was smooth and light. "She's resentful of anything that takes my attention away from her."

Lydia felt the impact of the words almost more than her ears heard them. There was a jerk like a giant pulse in her body, but she acted as though the meaning had not registered with her. "Nonsense," she declared. "I'm the furthest thing from the minds of her owners. Well, perhaps that's not wholly true. Fulvia has indicated to me that she would like to be friends."

Valleius' eyes studied her to see if her innocence was real. "I don't think Erosa cares one way or the other what Fulvia thinks or does. She cares very much about me."

Still Lydia feigned innocence. "Well, naturally. You're her owner, and so her welfare depends on your generosity."

Valleius laughed shortly. "I'm her owner and her god and she thinks no one else has any right to my thoughts."

"That must make difficulties for Fulvia," Lydia suggested.

"You persist in not understanding me. It's the way *you've* captured my thoughts that Erosa resents."

Lydia lowered her eyes but she kept her voice very gentle. "And I'm appreciative, sir. A widow is much in need of concern from those who can be kind."

Valleius' hand touched hers with a lingering caress. "I can be kinder to you than you'd ever believe possible."

To have ignored his touch and the insinuation of his words would have been ridiculous. Only a fool could mistake his meaning, and Lydia's pride would not permit her to play the fool for anyone. But how to answer him?

To act offended, to make a scene, to be prudish would only arouse the man's anger, and Lydia knew that his anger would be frightening, perhaps even dangerous.

"You're very kind," she murmured at last. "But, sir — Valleius —it's too soon. Surely you know that? I'm a woman who has been too deeply hurt too recently to even think of —pleasure."

She did not have to force the tears which filled her eyes. They were always ready to fall at the smallest word, the slightest memory.

"I don't want to make you cry," Valleius said in alarm. "I'm not a monster, surely."

"Aurelius was a wonderful man," Lydia said. "It would be dishonor to him if I even allowed my thoughts to drift elsewhere for —for a long time."

Her words seemed to promise something that she knew she had no intention of ever carrying out. But it was the only safe way she could think of to get out of the present situation.

Valleius was at once all courtesy and all sympathy. "I understand. Truly I do. I was letting my own impatience carry me faster than is proper. You'll forgive me, won't you?"

She wiped her eyes and smiled as warmly as possible. "Of course you're forgiven. I know I would be flattered if grief were not so close to my heart."

Valleius patted her arm. "I can be patient," he said. "Surely some day grief will disappear and you'll be free to enjoy life again."

She only smiled. The words, "What about Fulvia?" clamored to be said, but she held her tongue. Fulvia had indicated that night at their home that she knew Valleius was not faithful, and there was no point in antagonizing the man if it could be avoided. He had too much power in Philippi, too much influence in the Roman garrison for the seller of purple to risk his displeasure.

"But I do sometimes need help," Lydia confided in a soft voice. She was an honest woman and she did not enjoy using deceit, and yet she was a woman alone and had no other weapons at her disposal. "I'm worried about my son, and I need advice."

Valleius smiled benevolently. "If I know anything that will help you, I'll do what I can."

"He has taken to leaving the house at night," Lydia began.

"He's nearly a man," Valleius replied. "A man has needs a mother knows nothing of."

Lydia shook her head with emphasis. "No, he assures me there are no—no romantic activities involved. He's not meeting a girl. He's going to the garrison."

Valleius' eyebrows rose. "Does he want to be a soldier? I had guessed him to be a philosopher, a poet."

Something fell in place in Lydia's mind. Just hearing the words in the blunt male voice made something clear that had been eluding her.

"I think perhaps he is," she admitted slowly. "That is, I think his mind is that of a poet or philosopher. I suppose he thinks he *ought* to care only for games or battles. He never told me this, I'm only guessing."

Valleius nodded. "It's hardly anything a boy would admit to his mother."

"Perhaps he himself doesn't even realize it." Things were becoming clearer in Lydia's mind. "He says he wants the roughness of men in the garrison. He's never been awfully good at games, so he's never had much success in the competitions. But at the garrison he can be crude and vulgar, and he can feel more masculine."

"Probably. So why are you so concerned?"

"It just seems odd. Especially that he should go at night. People don't usually go out at night. And last evening was the first time he has even admitted to me that he was going out. Always before, he has been sneaking —slipping out without my knowledge."

Valleius noted the shift in words and grinned. "So what do you want from me? Do you want me to order him not to go to the garrison?"

"No, of course not." She spoke stiffly in spite of her resolution to be soft and feminine. "He's *my* son. I thought perhaps you could tell me something of one of the men there. A man that Ditus spoke about."

"What's his name?"

"Clement. I don't know the family name."

Valleius studied her shrewdly. "There's only one Clement that I know. He's the jailer."

"The jailer?"

Valleius noted her tone of voice with satisfaction. "Not a patrician, eh? Not the social class you'd choose for your son?"

"Is he a soldier?" she asked.

"Yes. Or was. He was injured in battle and limps, a spear wound, I understand. He can handle the jailer's work. And he always works at night. Maybe that explains why Ditus goes to the garrison after dark, when most people are in their beds."

"It seems odd that the man would always be on night duty," Lydia said.

"At his own request. There's family trouble, a sick wife or something, and he needs to be home during the day. Even sleeping, he's there where he can be reached if they need him."

"What kind of man is he?" Lydia asked. "Have you any idea why Ditus would seek him out?"

Valleius leaned back and stretched. "He's a decent enough fellow. Laughs a lot. Plays dice, I think. For some reason, people like him. There's always a small group gathered there. Almost like a party. Very innocent, I assure you. I suppose it keeps him from going mad there night after night listening to the prisoners howling in their chains."

Lydia could not help the shudder that shook her. "It seems a very strange choice for Ditus. He was brought up so—so—"

"Gently?" Valleius suggested, and his smile mocked her.

Lydia only shook her head helplessly. She couldn't think of a better word, and yet she knew Valleius' choice had been wrong.

"I would like to talk to this Clement," she murmured. "I'd like to know for myself what he's like."

"Your son will resent your intrusion," Valleius warned her. "But perhaps—if, say, you'd consent to see Erosa again, I could arrange that Clement would stop by your shop."

"That's blackmail, sir," she said indignantly.

He only smiled and waited.

"All right," she said at last. "I don't see what can be achieved, but I'll see her again. And perhaps—perhaps you could arrange it that I might see this Clement at *your* house. So Ditus won't know."

"I'll be glad to. A secret between two people always makes a sort of bond."

She ignored that and rose from the table. "I must start for home. The afternoon is going swiftly and it takes a long time to get to Philippi."

"It does indeed. Would you like me to accompany your carriage, now that you are carrying the precious load of purple?"

"I'm grateful for your concern, but I really think I'll be fine. I have trustworthy slaves, a good pair of horses, and the peace of Rome to protect me," she said. She thought he might insist on accompanying her, but he did not and she was able to say her farewell and start on her way.

It was only when she was traveling across the plain, following the Via Ignatia, that she thought of Reuben's god. If he were real, if he were all the things Reuben had said, then she had more than the peace of Rome to protect her. And at the thought, she felt a stillness begin to fill her, a stillness that dissolved her worries over Ditus and Valleius and the coming meeting with Erosa, a stillness that filled her with a kind of peace she had never known before, not even when Aurelius was alive.

8

Lydia arrived home only a little later than her usual time for getting back from the shop, and Minta was waiting for her.

"Did you come in a carriage?" Minta asked. "I thought I heard one stopping."

"Yes. I had to be away from Philippi on business." If she told Minta that she had gone to Neapolis, there would probably be a scene. Minta loved riding in the carriage, loved the seaport, loved anything that might lift her out of the routine of her days.

"Did you go far?" Minta asked, helping Lydia unwind the pallas from her head and shoulders.

"No, not far," Lydia answered, watching Minta fold the filmy material. "You're too young for a pallas, I suppose, but that material looks so pretty against your skin. Would you like to have it?"

"Oh, Mother!" Minta cried rapturously. "Do you mean it?"

"Would I say it if I didn't mean it?" Lydia asked sensibly. "Why don't you take it up to your room and put it away in your chest, then come down to the peristyle and we'll just sit for a few minutes before it's time to eat. I'm awfully tired."

Minta hugged her mother with appreciation and turned

to do as she was told. She was hardly out of the room when Ditus' voice caused Lydia to spin around.

"You don't plan to tell her, then, that you were in Neapolis all day?"

"She'd only be upset, Ditus. Why make trouble?"

"I don't suppose it occurred to you that you could have kept her out of school and taken her with you?" Ditus said.

"It occurred to me, yes," she answered resentfully, feeling as though she were being questioned in a court. "But what would I have done with her while I bargained with the shipowner? What impression would he have formed of me if I'd been accompanied by my child? He would have thought of me as a mother, not as a businesswoman."

"And what would you have done with her while you were with Valleius Tatinius?" Ditus asked in so quiet a tone that for a few seconds she did not recognize the words as accusation.

She felt herself flushing. "I would have welcomed her then."

Ditus said nothing, but his expression was frankly doubtful.

"Valleius is a man of power and influence in this town," Lydia said, hating it that she even felt the explanation was necessary. "His wife is going to be my friend, I hope. Valleius is a —a pleasant enough man, and it was to my advantage in a city away from home for a man to take me to the inn to eat."

"I could have served as escort," Ditus said.

Lydia's mouth dropped open in astonishment. "I never even thought of it," she admitted frankly. "I'm truly sorry. I don't think it even entered my head that you'd want to go, want to be with your mother all day."

Ditus stared at her for a moment. "I sometimes wonder if you ever think at all about what I would like."

"Ditus, that's not true. I think of you all the time. You're on my mind more than any other person, except possibly your father."

"And you think of us both with grief."

The statement was so true that Lydia could not refute it. She only stood looking at the boy, helpless and angry.

"I'm sorry," she said again. "I'm truly sorry."

But Ditus was persistent. "You can buy Minta's affection with exciting things like a grown woman's pallas, but you can't buy mine with apologies that cost you nothing," he declared, and oddly enough, his anger made him seem younger rather than older.

Lydia wondered if he realized this, and her heart twisted with pity.

"Ditus, please listen to me. Sit here, on this bench, and listen to me with as much fairness as you can manage," she begged.

He sat beside her, but gingerly, as though his body were poised for flight. "Listen," she said again. "I'm very troubled just now. You'll never know until you face the same thing how much I miss your father, how frightened I am at the idea of being alone, of being solely responsible for you and Minta. No, wait," she said as he started to interrupt. "Let me finish. I'm lonely and frightened and worried about the business. But I'm also excited and proud of some of the things I'm doing. You think of me only as your mother, but I'm a woman with feelings of my own that you can't understand."

"And I'm a man with feelings of my own that you can't understand."

"Not entirely a man," she argued. "You still have a lot of growing up to do. Do you have to blame *me* for the difficulties that you encounter?"

"I have to blame *someone*," he cried with such despair in his voice that she forgot her anger and felt only compassion.

She risked reaching over to touch his hand and for once, he did not jerk away from her.

"Life just doesn't make sense," Ditus said. "I wish I could be like some of my friends who care only about games and hunting and going to—to houses where girls are."

Lydia's heart plunged with a terrible fear. "Don't you like girls?" she whispered.

"Of course, I like girls. What do you think I am? But I don't want a girl I pay money for. I want—I want—" His words trailed off dismally.

"You want a girl to love," Lydia said and there was such a surge of thanksgiving in her heart that she had room for nothing but joy. She felt a foolish need to thank someone that Ditus was safe from the taint that had lain hidden behind all the other worries in her heart. But there was no one to thank. (No one? Maybe Jehovah, Reuben?) "You want a girl to love and marry and a profession that will give you satisfaction. It's just that it's too soon, can't you see? If your father hadn't died, you'd still be in school and not thinking of these things."

"But he *did* die," Ditus said flatly, "and I—I think life is senseless."

"I've thought so myself," she admitted. "I wonder if it would help any if you'd talk to Reuben?"

"And have him try to tell me all about that god of his? Gods are the most senseless part of life. If there was anything real or good about gods, they'd prevent such awful things from happening, things like my father dying and that slave of Valleius' being mad."

Lydia stared into his face, seeing the anger, the frustration, the fear. If only I were wiser, she thought, if I really had some kind of faith myself, maybe I could help this boy.

"Besides," Ditus added bitterly, "Jews have crazier ideas than most people. They think their god demands that all boy babies be circumcised. Did you know that?"

"Are you sure?" Lydia asked incredulously.

"Of course I'm sure. There was a Jew in my class at school. He tried to explain it but it sounded crazy to me. It still does."

Lydia hesitated. "Maybe there's a reason. I don't know. I don't know what that would have to do with the kind of belief Reuben seems to have. But, I'm impressed with the confidence he has, the faith. I'd like something like that myself."

Ditus looked alarmed. "You've got enough problems in your life," he said, "without getting involved with religion."

Maybe he was right, Lydia thought, but she said nothing.

"Well—" Ditus looked embarrassed. He probably hadn't intended to speak so frankly to his mother. "Well, do I have time to run down to the baths? I won't bother with anything else."

"I'll see that you have enough time," she said. "I'll have dinner held for you."

"Thanks. I'll hurry."

"And Ditus, life isn't really senseless. It's just difficult at times," she said, forgetting, for the moment, her own conviction of life's futility when Aurelius died.

He stood up. "I'm learning to laugh when things get hard," he confided. "I'm learning not to care."

That wasn't the answer either, she thought, but she didn't put the thought into words. "Next time," she promised, "next time I go to Neapolis, I'll ask you to go with me. You'd be a comfort to me."

"I doubt that Valleius Tatinius would think so," Ditus said brusquely and almost ran out of the peristyle toward the corridor that led to the street.

The conversation had been disturbing, Lydia thought, and yet there had been moments when she had felt there was hope for a healing in her relationship with her son.

But one thing had been very clear. Ditus shared Valleius'

opinion that she had been made so vulnerable by her loss that she would not be able to resist an attractive man. Perhaps, with patience, Ditus could be dissuaded, but Valleius was different. She would have to give much thought to the problem of Valleius.

Reuben was waiting for her the next day in the storeroom of the shop. He carefully unwrapped a bundle on the table. As the linen cloth fell away, Lydia saw that the package contained scrolls, very old and dark, and many more than she had expected.

"Are these all yours?" she asked.

"All mine. I won't tell you where I got them," he said darkly. "It's better that you don't know."

"Did you steal them?" She couldn't stop the question.

"It's better that you don't know," he repeated. "It's enough to say that I've had them for many years, that although they are stained and worn from my hands, I have been more careful of them than I am of the blood that flows in my body."

"So many," Lydia exclaimed. "There must be a number of books there. I expected only a few scrolls at most."

"I have almost all of the Torah," Reuben said proudly. "And there are portions of Isaiah and the psalms of King David. There are riches here, Lydia, riches beyond your comprehension."

None of the names he mentioned meant anything to her, but she caught at one of them. "Isaiah?" she asked. "What do you mean, you have 'portions of Isaiah'?"

"He was a prophet of the Jews hundreds of years ago. He wrote God's truth in a way that has lifted the hearts of men for centuries. I have the portion of his book that tells of the coming of the Messiah. His prophecy of a Messiah is the hope of our people and has been for generations."

She laughed a little. "I try to get one thing clarified and

you only add more confusion. What's a 'Messiah' and what has it to do with this Isaiah?''

Reuben shook his head. "I'm going too fast," he admitted. "Why don't you take the scrolls home and read them when you can? I think you'll understand more when you acquaint yourself with the prophecy and the poetry and the history of the Jewish nation."

"I don't read anything but Latin and Greek," she began. "If these are written in your native language...."

"They're in Greek," Reuben explained. "So many Jews came to Greece during the past centuries, so many have been born here, that it became necessary to put the Scripture into the language of the land."

She watched him re-wrap the scrolls. "All right," she conceded. "I love history and poetry, and if the prophesying isn't as frightening as Erosa's is, I expect I'll enjoy that, too."

"That girl still bothers you, doesn't she? I don't like that. Can't you just put her out of your mind?" he asked.

"It's not as easy as all that. Valleius wants me to see her again."

Reuben snorted. "Why don't you tell him that you absolutely refuse? That she bothers and frightens you."

"Valleius Tatinius is a powerful man," she said soberly. "You know that. You're surely aware of how much influence he exerts in this town and in the garrison. How would it go for us, do you think, if he told all his friends that Lydia the seller of purple was stupid, or a cheat, or that the cloth she sold was no longer worthwhile? We'd be lost, my friend."

Reuben scratched the side of his nose. "You might be right," he admitted. "That puts you in a position of great delicacy, doesn't it?"

"Of great delicacy," she agreed. She glanced over her shoulder. "But come, we've talked long enough. Ditus is scowling at us from the corner and I think I hear a customer in the stoa. We'd better get busy."

"Just —be very careful of the scrolls, won't you?"

"I'll guard them with my life," she answered and a sudden premonition of the scrolls' influence touched her like a drift of evening breeze, sweet and refreshing. She felt almost wholly confident when she turned toward the stoa, so the sight of Valleius standing in the opening off the street was like a sharp blow.

"Sir?" she said, her breath too ragged to shape more than the small word.

"I came only to deliver a message," he said. "You needn't look so upset. It's just a simple message. Or," he laughed lightly, "maybe not so simple since it has three parts."

"Three?"

"Yes. Fulvia asked me to tell you she would stop by the shop sometime today. Just to make plans for another meeting, she said. And second, Erosa will come here to see you today at noon if you'll permit it. You'll be more comfortable in your own surroundings, I think, and there won't be any customers at that time."

"I suppose I can see her," Lydia said stiffly.

"I've kept my part of the bargain, too," he said in a conspiratorial tone. "If you'll stop by our house this afternoon when you leave work, most people, including my wife, will be at the baths, and you can meet the friend you want to know."

"You're sure he'll be there?" Lydia searched Valleius' face to try to determine if he were being completely honest.

"You think I'd deceive you? No, my dear, I don't work that way. I'm a patient man, and a man of honor. If I say I'll keep my half of a bargain, I'll keep it."

"Thank you. I'll stop by. And tell Fulvia that I look forward to her coming."

Valleius bent his head in acknowledgment and turned to leave. In turning, he saw Ditus at the door of the storeroom. "Ah, Ditus!" Valleius called out. "My greetings on this bright day!"

The expression on Ditus' face was surly, but he gave Valleius a formal greeting and turned to his work table.

"He wasn't much friendlier than that yesterday," Valleius confided with a twinkle. "Do you suppose he suspects ulterior motives?"

Lydia ignored the queston. "Good-bye, sir," she said, and turned to serve a customer who had entered the stoa. With an abrupt wave, Valleius left and Lydia began the work of the day, knowing with dread that noontime would come all too soon.

9

The stoa had been empty of customers for only a few minutes when Lydia looked up to see Nuba and Erosa standing in the street. She couldn't see Valleius anywhere, but she was delighted to discover Fulvia hurrying toward her along the colonnaded porch.

"My master sent us, my lady," Nuba began, but Fulvia came up to him and touched his arm with an arresting motion.

"I'm here, Nuba," she said. "Lydia, my greetings."

Lydia's relief at seeing Fulvia instead of Valleius must have shown on her face, but she could not help the gladness that surged up in her.

"And greetings to you, dear Fulvia," she cried. "Here, come in out of the sun. And, Nuba, you, too. Bring Erosa in here where there's shade, where it's cooler."

For a few minutes, there was only the bustle of seeing that everyone was seated, then a small silence fell.

"My master sent us," Nuba began again. "He said he'd meet us here, but Erosa begged to come early."

Lydia smiled into the slave's black eyes. "I'm surprised your master lets you out alone with Erosa. Doesn't he worry?"

Nuba lifted his head with pride. "He trusts me entirely," he said. He turned to the girl who sat in silence beside him.

"Well, you're here," he said. "If you want to say anything to the lady before the master comes, you'd better hurry."

Erosa got up and moved over to where Lydia sat on one of the stools. Still in silence, the girl knelt and lifted one of Lydia's hands in her own. "May I, my lady?" she asked. "Or must I wait for my master?"

Lydia looked into the large, dark eyes so close to her own. They neither glittered with madness nor were they veiled sleepily with rounded lids. If there was anything in the depths of Erosa's eyes that Lydia could recognize, it was a spark of maliciousness. She had seen it often enough in her own slaves to recognize it.

"Please go ahead," Lydia said. "To be truthful, I'd prefer not to have a man around while you tell my fortune."

"Not your fortune, my lady," Erosa said in such a calm, sane voice that Lydia felt bewildered. It was almost as if this weren't the same girl who had screeched and struggled that night in Valleius' house. "Not your fortune, but your future. They aren't the same."

Lydia only nodded, wanting the girl to get on with what she had to say so that she would go away.

Erosa took Lydia's hand, and while the small fingers were cool, they were not deathly cold as they had been the first time. It seemed as though whatever demon possessed this small person, it had left her in relative peace for the moment.

"Your hand is an empty one," Erosa announced, but the look she slid toward Lydia's face was sly rather than intense. "You are meant to be alone. To make friends, with a man I mean, will be wrong for you. I see you growing old alone, dignified and successful —but *alone*."

There was definite warning in her voice, and Lydia felt herself relaxing. A jealous slave was nothing to be afraid of, and in fact, Erosa's jealousy might be the very thing Lydia needed as a weapon. How easy it would be to say, "What if Erosa should see you coming to my shop? Perhaps you should not risk angering her, or the demon that possesses her."

So Lydia found herself smiling down at the little slave with a feeling of kindness. "If you promise me dignity," she murmured, "then evidently I won't be too lonely and I'll be able to face this solitary life you see for me."

The girl's eyes were suspicious of Lydia's compliance. "I haven't finished, my lady," she remonstrated.

"Sorry," Lydia said politely.

Fulvia had remained silent, but her eyes were watching Erosa shrewdly and a grim little smile pulled at the corners of her mouth.

Erosa's voice took on a deeper resonance. "In fact, I see great tragedy for you if you seek out a man's company, even for friendship. No, that's wrong. You may safely, I think, be friends with the men you work with in your business, but no others. You will risk great tragedy, greater trouble than any you've ever known. Do you understand?"

She looked sharply up at Lydia, and Lydia knew that every word Erosa said stemmed from her jealous desire to keep Valleius' affection and attention entirely for herself. There was no gift of divination in the girl at this moment.

"I understand," Lydia said gently. "Is that all you have to tell me?"

Erosa continued to kneel, staring at Lydia, and it seemed as though she wanted to look away but couldn't. She even made a feeble attempt to scramble up from her knees, but her body jerked into rigidness, and her eyes glazed over with madness. Lydia felt the small fingers holding hers turn clammy and cold.

"You are searching for a belief, aren't you?" Erosa said in a voice so different from the one she had just been using that it might have been another girl talking. "Well, you'll find it, you'll find it soon, but it will bring you sorrow and difficulty when all you're looking for is comfort."

Her sudden change had drawn them all into a spell, and

none of them were aware that Valleius had stepped into the stoa at the same instant that Reuben entered it from the storeroom. Both men stood for a minute staring at the scene in front of them.

"Why did you let her come early?" Valleius hissed to Nuba.

The slave jumped a little, tearing his eyes away from Erosa. "She insisted, Master. Would you have had me wait until she was hysterical? It's all right. Nothing has happened."

"Lydia," Reuben said sharply, ignoring Valleius' angry motion for silence. "Lydia, may I speak to you?"

Lydia, caught and held by the mad eyes, seemed unable to move her head toward the old man.

"Lydia!" Reuben spoke louder. "Look at me."

But it was Erosa who looked at him, and an expression of utter terror spread over her face. "If you listen to him," she shrieked to Lydia, "he'll tell you of the Most High God, the one true God. Don't listen to *him*."

"Be quiet!" Reuben thundered. "Don't blaspheme the name of my God with your babble."

Erosa shrank back, and her face went totally blank. The madness was gone and so were the slyness and purpose which had brought her to Lydia's shop. She looked around in a dazed way. "I want to go home," she whimpered. "Nuba, take me home."

"You were the one who insisted on coming," Valleius said with irritation.

Lydia had to wet her lips before she could speak. "I think she has said what she wanted to say. She was prophesying to me quite a while before you came, and prophesying with skill, I'd say."

"And you're not upset by her?" Valleius asked.

"No, not at all. Her words weren't exactly comforting,

but they contained a warning for me. I'll abide by it, I think. There's no use taking chances."

Reuben and Valleius both looked puzzled. "I'm not talking about the last thing she said," Lydia explained. "There was more."

"More?"

"It was private, if you don't mind."

"I want to go home," Erosa whimpered again, and she seemed to shrink away from Reuben.

"May I take her, Master?" Nuba asked.

Valleius seemed to hesitate and then, glancing at Lydia, he shrugged. "Yes, take her home. I'll walk with you. Are you coming, my dear?" he added to Fulvia.

"No, thank you. Not for a few minutes. I have one of the slaves to accompany me, and I want to talk to Lydia."

Valleius bowed curtly to the two women, completely ignored Reuben, and started home, shepherding Erosa and Nuba before him.

For a few seconds, there was silence in the stoa. Lydia thought surely Fulvia would comment about Erosa's pretense at prophecy, which had been such an obvious attempt to warn Lydia away from Valleius.

But when Fulvia spoke, it was not to Lydia at all. She turned to Reuben: "She was right, wasn't she?" Fulvia said with quiet conviction. "Your God is the Most High God—the one true God."

"He is," Reuben said stiffly, "but to hear him named by a mad pagan is blasphemy."

"Will you tell me about him?" Fulvia said humbly, as though Reuben had not spoken. "Will you teach me?"

Reuben looked at her and then glanced at Lydia. There was a silence, as though everyone in the room needed time to catch up with the sudden turn of events. Then Lydia smiled at the old man. "We'll plan to eat here each day as we did yesterday, and then, my dear old friend, you'll have a class for two. We can study the scrolls together. Would that please you?''

"The Lord be praised!" Reuben exulted. "The Lord be praised forever and forever."

When she left work that afternoon, Lydia turned, as she had promised to do, toward the Tatinius home. The apprehension she had felt all day was not helped by the fact that she felt weary and mussed. She wished she had planned to stop at the baths first so she could have felt more confident about meeting this man, Clement.

A border of brilliant poppies edged the street and almost as though they had spoken to her, Lydia reminded herself that there was a bright side to her situation. Fulvia had promised to stay home from the baths so she could come down after Lydia had talked to Clement a short time.

"It'll give you a perfect excuse if the man is a boor," Fulvia had said, and Lydia had welcomed the suggestion.

How lovely, Lydia reflected, giving the poppies another appreciative glance, to have a friend who understood one's problems.

There was another pleasant thing to think about, Lydia reflected. Tomorrow was Reuben's Sabbath, and he had promised that both Lydia and Fulvia could go with him to the place by the Gangites River outside the city walls where the Philippian Jews worshipped. There weren't enough men to make a proper congregation, Reuben had explained, but there were some women and a few men, and Lydia and Fulvia could listen and learn.

Just before turning into the street that led to the Tatinius home, Lydia had another happy thought. While she was talking to the man, Clement, her slave Pyrus could be sent home to bring Minta and Sidri so that after the meeting, they could all go to the baths together. The weariness and worry of the day could be washed away. Minta would like that and so would she.

Feeling easier in mind, Lydia hurried to Valleius' house. He met her at the door, and she had a moment of panic. Had he gotten her here under false pretenses?

But Valleius only murmured "How good to see you again!" before he led her to the peristyle where a man waited.

"This is Mistress Lydia, seller of purple," Valleius introduced her. "Lydia, this is Clement, a soldier at the garrison."

Clement came toward them. He wasn't tall, not a great deal taller than Lydia herself, but he was broad and strong looking. He walked with a limp, but there was nothing about him which marked him as a cripple. His eyes blazed with life, but crinkled at the corner. His face was the face of a man who laughed frequently; his mouth seemed flexible and ready to smile.

He bowed. "Greetings, Mistress Lydia. I'm honored."

She felt suddenly uncomfortable and recognized the reason. She was here on an errand of deceit.

But Clement was apparently a stranger to deceit. "The Magistrate tells me that you're concerned about your son," Clement said abruptly.

Lydia looked helplessly at Valleius. She certainly hadn't expected so frank an approach.

"Shall we all sit down?" Valleius asked. "And may I have some wine brought?"

"For the lady if she wishes," Clement said, oddly in control of the situation although he was not a patrician in appearance. "But not for me. I'm needed at home and can only stay for as long as it's necessary to tell Mistress Lydia what she wants to know."

"Then by all means, don't let me hold you back with pleasantries. I'll leave you here so that you can talk. I'll be in the atrium if you need me," Valleius said, and strode away.

Lydia and Clement sat on benches facing one another.

"No doubt you think me a very foolish mother," Lydia began.

"All mothers are a little foolish," Clement said with a smile.

She looked intently at him. "What did Valleius tell you?" she demanded.

He shrugged good naturedly. "Only that you wanted to know what Ditus was doing at night when he left the house."

"Well," she said, "what *is* he doing?"

She hadn't intended to be so abrupt, but the man made her ill at ease with his amiable attitude toward this problem that deviled her.

Clement laughed. "Nothing you'd want to share, Mistress Lydia. He's becoming a remarkably good gambler, but never for much more than a few sesterii. None of us can afford large stakes. He's learning to listen to a bawdy story without blushing like a girl. He's learning that if you laugh, things don't hurt so much."

His first words had made her bristle and sit erect, but his final statement stopped the hot, hasty words she had planned to say.

"I'm not sure that laughing is always the answer," she said.

He shrugged again. "Nevertheless, I've found it so."

She stared at him curiously. "Your wife is ill?" she ventured. "Valleius said your wife's illness makes it necessary for you to work at night."

He shifted on his seat with embarrassment. "Don't get the idea that I'm a devoted nursemaid," he said gruffly. "I'm not. Our married daughter lives with us; her husband is a soldier in the garrison, and he is willing to live with his wife's family, so she takes care of my wife. But if I can be in the house during the day, it makes things easier for the girl. Sometimes, my wife is hard to manage. The pain, you know..."

Lydia studied his face. "And with that situation, you still find life is something to laugh at?"

"What good would it do me to cry?" he asked.

"Maybe that's why Ditus seeks you out," Lydia said. "Maybe he's seen all the weeping he can stand."

"Maybe. I've never asked him."

"But he gambles, you say?" Lydia persisted.

"And getting good at it, too," Clement said, and there was pride in his voice. "He's a boy who won't catch much attention with his skill in games; he's not much of a runner or wrestler. But his brain is clever, sharp. So he can throw dice and curse as well as any man."

"It doesn't seem anything to be proud of," Lydia protested.

"It all depends on who's looking at him," Clement said. "Me, I think he's good."

"Well, if it's no worse than what you say, I suppose I can live with it," Lydia said doubtfully.

Clement shrugged again. His smile was amiable, and his elbows rested on his knees. Everything about the man was casual and accepting.

What a comfort this must be to Ditus. Lydia thought with a sudden sense of revelation. How reassuring to be accepted on such a simple basis.

"Then I suppose I shouldn't object any longer. Or demand that he tell me where he's going," Lydia said.

Clement grinned. "You'd spoil all his fun."

"I beg your pardon?"

"Half the joy for him is in thinking he's going against the rules. You don't want to spoil that, do you?"

Lydia looked perplexed. "You mean you think I ought to pretend I'm still worried about him."

"And well you should be, shouldn't you? Gambling with

a bunch of ruffians is hardly the way a young gentleman should spend his time. And if you'd hear his language, you'd hold your ears." The tone was playful, but she knew he was not mocking her.

"I don't understand you," she said helplessly.

"You don't know me," Clement responded, and the simple words brought her eyes up to his.

For a long minute, they stared at each other, and Lydia was conscious of her heart beating. She felt an inexplicable desire to contradict him, to say she did know him in some strange way.

"You go on worrying and making rules," Clement advised. "I'll teach him how to throw the dice and how to laugh. We'll be working at cross purposes, maybe, or so it'll seem. But out of it will come a man we can be proud of, I shouldn't wonder."

The advice was given in the same calm, kind, reassuring way that Aurelius had used. Lydia felt something relaxing in her, something that had been knotted tightly ever since Aurelius' death.

"Thank you," she whispered.

"Thank *you*," he said, "for paying me the honor of listening to my suggestion."

Fulvia came into the room and Lydia realized that she was sorry to see her. How odd, when she had been counting on Fulvia's arrival as a means of escape.

"Then I'll leave," Clement said. He bowed a little awkwardly to both women and limped away.

And Lydia, watching, felt only regret at seeing him go.

She turned to Fulvia. "I have to meet Minta," she said, "and go to the baths with her. Will you tell your husband I'm grateful?"

"Are you really? Was it all right?"

"Yes." She wanted to leave before Valleius could return. "I'll tell you all about it tomorrow. Farewell, my friend."

Fulvia nodded. "Farewell. I'll meet you in the morning, an hour after sunrise. By the library, did we say?"

Lydia nodded and hurried to the door in time to see Minta and Sidri coming down the street toward her. All at once, Lydia was terribly glad to see her daughter. She was filled with the maternal warmth that had seemed to escape her lately. It's Clement, she thought with amazement. He's like Aurelius in some mysterious, comforting way.

10

The Gangites River flowed through a tree-lined valley about a mile west of Philippi. The grassy, shaded river banks were cool and fresh smelling after the long walk across the dusty plain. Lydia and Fulvia, who had walked there together, sat and listened to the sounds of praise that flowed from the worshiping Jews gathered near them. There were only four men, and they sat apart from the women, with shawls thrown over their heads, their eyes closed, and their faces serene.

There had been some attempt to make this open place by the river look a little like a temple. A small box made of wood with a curtain that shielded its contents rested on the ground, and beside it on a level stone was a seven-branched lamp. A screen stood behind it to protect the flames from the breeze that whispered over the water. It was odd, Lydia thought, how these small items seemed to create an atmosphere of dignity.

Reuben was the oldest man present, and Lydia expected him to be the one who would read from the scroll that was revealed when the curtain of the box was lifted. But it was a boy who stood to read, a boy not much older than Ditus. He was straight and slim, and his voice rose and fell in a chant that carried the words to Lydia in a wave of loveliness.

"Who is the man who fears the Lord?" the boy chanted.

103

"He will instruct him in the way he should choose. His soul will abide in prosperity, and his descendants will inherit the land. *The secret of the Lord is for those who fear him, and he will make them know his covenant.*"

The words were so filled with promise and hope that Lydia found herself leaning forward to hear better. Beside her, Fulvia also seemed to strain toward the reader.

"My eyes are continually toward the Lord," the boy went on, "for he will pluck my feet out of the net. Turn to me and be gracious to me, for I am lonely and afflicted. The troubles of my heart are enlarged; bring me out of my distresses."

Oh, yes, Lydia thought. I *am* lonely and afflicted. Dare I ask this Lord to hear me?

Her thoughts made her lose the next bit of what was read, but the final words came clearly to her. "Guard my soul and deliver me; do not let me be ashamed, for I take refuge in thee. Let integrity and uprightness preserve me, for I wait for thee. Redeem Israel, O God, out of all his troubles."

The boy carefully re-wrapped the scroll and sat down beside the other men. One of them began to sing in a minor chant, a song of praise, and the entire congregation, including the women, joined in the phrases of affirmation and in the Amens.

Lydia and Fulvia exchanged a glance.

Fulvia whispered, "Have you ever seen anything like this before?"

Lydia shook her head. "No sacrifices," she whispered back. "No statues. No —orgies. Only this —what? This praising."

One of the women glanced at them, and they were silent with a sudden feeling of guilt.

Just when Lydia had decided that Reuben was apparently going to have nothing to do with this service, he began to speak. He did not stand but remained seated on the ground, his hands resting quietly in his lap, his head covered by the shawl that shaded his face so that he seemed almost a stranger.

"David has read one of the psalms of King David. In it, he read of the Lord's covenant, of our need for forgiveness, and of the mercy that is available for those who fear the Lord. There is for us, in this small portion of God's holy word, a promise, an admonition, and a hope."

The small group was silent and all eyes were fixed on Reuben's face.

"Without walls to shelter us or an ark to hold the precious scrolls, without a priest to serve us, we are yet gathered in the name of the Lord of Hosts," Reuben said. "And I, most humble of all rabbis, with so small a flock that we cannot even call this a synagogue, I take this Sabbath time to talk to you about the hope and the assurance of the covenant that God has made with his chosen people."

Lydia's attention was fully riveted on Reuben, and for perhaps an hour she listened to him talk. She failed to understand much of what he said, and more than once she and Fulvia exchanged questioning glances, but there were occasional moments when the truth seemed to glow with an incredible brilliance.

The most impressive part of all, Lydia reflected, was that there was nothing here that was like any of the other religions she knew. There was nothing similar to the worship of Jupiter or Dionysius or Isis, nothing to reflect the usual Roman obsession with the stars. There was only this fixed and single idea, that God *was*, that he ruled the world, that he was gracious and merciful, and that in return, his believers must be decent and honest and kind. She marveled that this handful of people, far from their native land, isolated from their own temples and priests, could hold so firmly and unwaveringly to their own belief, that it had not been colored at all by the other religions that surrounded it.

When Reuben finished his talk, there was another song.

As the people stood, Lydia and Fulvia scrambled up from the ground and waited awkwardly, not knowing what to do next. The gathering turned as one to face east, and one of the men who had not yet spoken began to pray in a strong, beseeching voice.

"Hear us, O Lord, hear your children's cry," he said. "Grant unto us your shelter and your peace. Bless us and strengthen us and make us one. For thou only, O Lord, are mighty and able to preserve our going out and our coming in. To thee we turn, O Lord, to thee we pray on this holy day."

There was silence for a minute, and Lydia felt a prayer quivering in the center of her body. "Oh, yes, Lord," she thought achingly, "bless me and keep me and preserve me."

She forgot to preface her prayer with the stipulation, "*If* there be such a god," so easily and so softly did she take the final step into belief.

The people spoke as one, a rush of voices shaping the words with familiarity and love: "Hear, O Israel, the Lord our God, the Lord is one."

The young boy who had read from the scrolls quietly and firmly repeated the words Reuben had said that day in the shop, "The Lord bless you and keep you. The Lord make his face to shine upon you. The Lord lift up his countenance upon you and give you peace. Amen."

Lydia had not planned to echo the Amen out loud, but she heard her voice chiming in with all the others, heard Fulvia's voice also saying the word. Lydia lifted her hands to scrub away tears on her cheek, embarrassed and disturbed, until she saw that Fulvia's cheeks were also wet.

"Silly of me to cry," Lydia said.

"Not so silly," Fulvia objected. "We've just heard what I've been looking for all my life."

"I, too," Lydia agreed, "but I guess I hadn't been aware of it. Not the way you were."

"You may not have been as hungry," Fulvia said, smiling,

"but I expect you'll appreciate the sensation of being filled as much as I."

A sturdy, strong woman came toward them. "I'm Miriam," she said. "Daughter of Jonah, widow of Jacob and mother of David. May I bid you welcome."

Lydia smiled and answered in the same way, identifying herself with the men in her life. "I'm Lydia, widow of Aurelius, mother of Epaphroditus. This is my friend Fulvia, wife of Valleius Tatinius and the mother of five or six sons."

Miriam's laughter was musical. "You're both welcome. Did you come just to observe us?"

"Oh, no," Lydia said hastily. "Reuben invited us. We—I'm coming to believe your God is the true God."

"He's the only God," Miriam corrected gently. "There's a difference."

Fulvia nodded. "We're learning that. It's hard to accept it all at once when we've always thought of dozens of gods."

"And that's as hard for me to imagine," Miriam replied. "The Shema was one of the first sentences I learned to say as a child; it was one of the first things I taught to David and to his sisters."

"The Shema?" Lydia asked.

"That sentence we all said together at the end. Hear, O Israel, the Lord our God, the Lord is one."

"And you teach your religious concepts to your children even as babies?" Fulvia asked.

"How else?" Miriam looked astonished. "They are children of the covenant."

The people were beginning to move away after they had packed the scroll into the box and put the lamp beside it. Lydia watched with some surprise as young David placed the articles into a hollow place at the foot of a tree, covering them carefully with branches.

"Why don't you just take the things with you?" Lydia asked.

"Because we don't carry heavy objects on the Sabbath,"

Miriam answered. "He'll come after sundown to get them."
She laughed softly. "You may be in the process of becoming
a God-fearer, but you have much to learn about what it
means to be a Jew."

"We don't know nearly enough about being a God-fearer,
as you call it, but Reuben's going to teach us."

"And if you'll come next Sabbath, you'll be welcome,"
Miriam assured them.

"Thank you," Fulvia said. "We'll be here."

Lydia and Fulvia walked slowly back to Philippi. They
talked of the things Reuben had said, of the words David
had read from the scroll, and of the solemnity of the prayer
which had been offered. The longer they talked, the more
enthusiastic they felt.

"This could become my life," Lydia confessed as they
walked through the gates and past the Roman garrison.

"I know. I feel the same. What a comfort that this belief,
this conviction has come to both of us. How lonely it would
be to have no one with whom one could talk about it."

Lydia only smiled. They were past the garrison now, and
were going along the street where the soldiers' quarters
were. Almost automatically the slaves, who had accompanied the women to the river, quickened their pace so that
they were walking closer to their mistresses.

Suddenly, terrible screams filled the air. Lydia didn't hear
the thud of a whip, so it couldn't be a slave or a prisoner
screaming like that. And it wasn't a child. It was obviously a
woman, even though the screams were almost bestial.

"Father!" A young woman's voice could be heard coming
clearly from one of the quarters. "Father, hurry, I can't hold
her."

"I'm coming. Hang on, girl, I'm coming."

Lydia had heard Clement's voice only once, but the sound
of it was shockingly familiar.

Averting her face and taking Fulvia's arm, Lydia hurried

along the street, hardly able to breathe for the horror which choked her.

Fulvia shuddered. "What was that, do you think?"

"A woman in pain. The wife of the man, Clement, I met at your house. She's dreadfully ill, I understand."

"Are you sure?"

"I recognized his voice. And I know that's why he works at night so he can be home during the day," Lydia explained.

"It would be a mercy if she died," Fulvia said.

But Lydia could not bring herself to echo the words. She knew too well the bitterness of being alone, although Clement was undoubtedly already suffering his own form of aloneness and pain.

The weeks went by. Minta, attracted by the things Lydia told her about the worship services by the river, accompanied her mother on the Sabbath morning excursions outside the city gates. To Lydia's astonishment, the girl embraced the whole idea. At first, Lydia thought it was only a childish infatuation for the young David who read from the scrolls each Sabbath. But in time she knew it was a solemn conviction that seemed to bring a solace and strength to Minta, turning her all at once into a young woman who was a source of companionship and comfort to Lydia, rather than a source of worry.

And each evening, Lydia brought home the new stories and laws that Reuben had taught her that day. Minta was eager for the information so that the dinner hour, like the lunch hour, evolved into a time of instruction and learning.

Ditus was obviously resentful and made more and more excuses to be absent from the evening meal. Lydia promised herself that she would talk about other subjects, ones in which Ditus would be interested, but Minta's eagerness and curiosity always drew her back to the things that Reuben had said at noon.

"It's worse than being in school," Ditus said bitterly one evening at dinner.

"But I thought you were the one who was interested in philosophy," Minta argued.

"Philosophy, yes," Ditus said. "This isn't philosophy you two are talking about. Philosophy allows for two points of view. You're both positive that there's only one point of view —yours."

"I suppose that's the difference between conjecture and faith," Lydia said, trying to be fair. "What was once a faint possibility to me has become a fact. That's all."

"Well, it bores me," Ditus said.

"If you'd listen," she said tartly, "maybe you'd benefit from the things we say. From what I can see of the life you lead, you could stand some moral improvement."

The boy was silent, staring at her. "I always tell you when I go out," he said sullenly.

"And where you go," she agreed. "But do you think it's anything to be proud of?"

"I bring no shame to this house," he argued.

"Nor any pride either," she retorted and was instantly contrite. "I'm sorry," she cried. "I didn't mean that."

Ditus was white. "You must have meant it or you wouldn't have said it."

Lydia stretched her hand toward her son. "I was angry. I spoke in anger. Of course I'm proud of you and what you're doing at the shop. I'm proud of both of my children. It's just . . ."

"It doesn't matter," Ditus said, getting up from the couch. "If you'll excuse me. I'm—I'm going out."

Going to the healing of Clement who accepts you as you are, Lydia thought. Why can't I accept you as you are and not constantly want you to be something you aren't?

"Be careful," she said as calmly as she could. "The streets are very dark."

"My slave carries a light," Ditus said.

Without a backward glance, the boy strode out of the room, his heels hitting hard on the stone floor.

"He feels I've deserted him," Minta explained in a little, lost voice. "And I guess I have. He doesn't trust me anymore."

"He doesn't trust me either," Lydia said ruefully. "And I dare not tell him that I trust him."

Minta looked at her with wide eyes.

"I know more of Ditus' activities than he realizes," Lydia confessed to her daughter. "But I think he needs my opposition so that he can —well—nurture himself on defiance."

Minta reached to pat her mother's hand. "Poor Mother," she said as though Lydia were the child. "Poor Mother who has to be as wise as a father and as loving as a mother. *And* support us by working every day. How do you do it?"

Lydia laughed mirthlessly. "I don't know. I don't think I've been very successful so far. If I didn't have Kora who knows how to run the house without daily instruction from me, I just don't know what I'd do. There are many who think I should be at home instead of in the shop. No, don't shake your head; you were one of them in the beginning. And I don't really possess much wisdom where Ditus is concerned. What little I have, I got from—" She stopped abruptly. It would never do to reveal her meeting with Clement to Minta.

"From Father. I know." Minta's soft patting continued. "But, Mother, we're not alone, you know. We have God to guide us and protect us."

Lydia looked gratefully at the girl beside her. "I know. I wish I didn't have to be reminded."

Minta smiled and their hands clasped warmly.

The slave, Kora, came to the door and spoke quietly. "Mistress, the Magistrate Valleius Tatinius waits in the atrium to see you."

Lydia had a spasm of nervousness, but before she could answer, Minta stood up.

"I'll just go up to my room," the girl said. "Will you ask Sidri to join me?" she added to Kora. Dropping a kiss on her mother's cheek, she ran from the room.

Lydia wanted to call her back but what possible excuse could she give? And besides, there may not be any need for Minta's presence. Perhaps Valleius only brought a message from Fulvia.

"Tell Magistrate Tatinius I'll be right in," she said, slipping her bare feet into the sandals Kora stooped to hold for her.

"Yes, my lady," Kora said, looking up. It was the curiosity and conjecture in Kora's dark eyes that heightened Lydia's apprehension. Kora had a genius for discovering the errand of each visitor, but she evidently did not know why Valleius had come after dark to Lydia's door.

11

Valleius was standing by the wedding couch, fingering the fringe on one of the cushions. When he heard Lydia's sandals whispering across the floor, he drew back quickly.

The wedding couch was a symbol in a home, Lydia thought with a quick surge of resentment, a symbol of the love and loyalty that ought to be part of every marriage, and Valleius had no right to touch the cushion that had once pillowed her head. Hers and Aurelius'.

She made her voice calm and friendly. "Valleius. What brings you to my door so late? Is Fulvia all right?"

Valleius' smile shifted into a scowl. "I'm beginning to think I should never have introduced Fulvia to you. It would have been better if you had remained strangers."

"Oh, no," Lydia cried, "her friendship means too much to me. I just don't know what I would have done these past months without her."

"Perhaps *I* might have found a way to comfort you," Valleius suggested.

"A woman needs another woman to listen and advise," Lydia said, and she knew her voice sounded prim. She didn't want to be prim, she thought. She wanted to be cool and logical and wise.

"But even more, my dear, a woman needs a man," Valleius argued. "Surely you know that." He came very close to her and tentatively touched her cheek.

She was unprepared for the way her heart lurched at his touch. How could she have forgotten the curious alchemy that existed between a woman and a man? Her grieving for Aurelius must have made her think that Aurelius had been the only man who had ever stirred her. Now, at Valleius' touch, she remembered the way she had felt as a girl when a boy had held her hand or looked deeply into her eyes. She had been inexperienced and silly then, which had explained the way her heart had raced. But what rendered her so vulnerable now? Loneliness, she supposed, and the undeniable fact that Valleius was a vital and attractive man.

She turned her face away from his hand, but gently so that he would not be offended. "Not every woman, my friend."

Valleius laughed, and she saw that his eyes were brilliant in the flickering light. Thank goodness, Kora had lit every lamp in the atrium, but that still left dark corners and shifting shadows.

"Oh, come now." Valleius captured her hand firmly and drew her toward a bench opposite the wedding couch. "Don't play games, Lydia. You know I've been very patient. It's been a long time since Aurelius died, and you must be very lonely. Wouldn't you let me —appease that loneliness, so to speak?"

He was very close and she found herself almost mesmerized by the glitter in his eyes.

"Sweet Lydia," he whispered and his mouth came down on hers.

The shock of his kiss ran like fire through her body, and she was astonished at the will she had to exert to keep her lips from softening and responding to his. It would be so easy, she thought with dismay, to just melt against him. It would be gratifying to feed her own hunger with this man's obvious admiration. But somehow she kept her lips from softening.

"So cool?" Valleius murmured, pulling back a little. "You're not a cool woman, Lydia. I can tell. Do you find me so distasteful?"

"What woman could find a Roman Magistrate—and a handsome one at that—distasteful?" Lydia said lightly, but her voice trembled in spite of herself.

"Apparently you can," Valleius said flatly. She was sure that he had not been unaware of the trembling.

"Not distasteful, my friend. But—your wife is my closest friend. What kind of a person would I be if I—if I—"

"Had her husband as a lover," Valleius said abruptly. "Why not?"

"Valleius, may I speak candidly?" Lydia asked, casting about in her mind for the right words.

"Why not?" he murmured and his eyes burned into hers.

"My mother was a woman of great virtue," Lydia began. "I was born and raised, you know, in the East where girls are reared with greater strictness than Roman girls are. My mother taught me that one gave oneself only in marriage."

Valleius laughed. "Dear little prude," he teased. "Of course, when you were sixteen or so, that was the only thing to believe. What else could keep you safe? But you're no longer sixteen. I would guess you're closer to thirty-five.

"Thirty-seven," she corrected.

Valleius looked at her with delight. "That's one of the things I love about you; you're as factual as a man but as fragrant as a woman."

Once more his lips came down on hers, and once more she had to suppress the shock of excitement that ran through her.

"Now what?" Valleius said with irritation. "Why are you still so cold?"

"We haven't solved the problem of Fulvia," Lydia said stubbornly, "How would I face—how *will* I face her knowing her husband has kissed me?"

"Fulvia's a very understanding wife," Valleius said. "She's never demanded total fidelity. She's surely aware of how lovely you are, how desirable. She wouldn't mind."

"How little you know women," Lydia retorted. "If you were my husband, I should mind very much."

"Oh, come. When Aurelius was living, you surely didn't expect him to be wholly faithful?"

"Oh, but I did. And he was."

"How do you know?"

A look came and went on his face that Lydia recognized as cruelty. He licked his lips, and as clearly as though he'd said the words, she knew he wanted to make up a tale about Aurelius' infidelity and taunt her with it. But no doubt he was afraid that would turn this into a scene of weeping and hysteria which would totally defeat his purpose.

"I just know," she said.

"But I love you," Valleius argued. "I've loved you since the day I came into the shop to buy the purple. I've been astonishingly patient for a man of my nature. How long do you expect me to wait?"

"You love me, you say." Lydia kept her voice very steady but the next words were shaped with risk. "Do you plan to divorce Fulvia then? Are you asking me to marry you?"

Valleius moved away from her and squinted, staring at her in the shifting light. "Are you serious?"

"I only wondered," she said, allowing the primness to fill her voice again.

"You're teasing me," Valleius said after studying her. "You're a woman who has known love —and the pleasures of a man. I could make you very happy. I could keep you from being lonely."

For a few seconds, the sheer logic of what he was saying appealed to her. There was no denying the fact that at times her body craved a man. And certainly she was not ready to think of remarriage, even if there were any widowers of her age who might appeal to her —which there weren't. And Valleius was right; Fulvia need not know.

Valleius, watching her face, seemed to understand the thoughts that were racing through her head.

"See, little love," he said softly, close to her face, "It would be so easy to just let go, and let me teach you how to love again."

His hands slid up her arms and drew her toward him. And for a second she went, pliant and soft.

The memory of the words of the law seemed to explode inside her head. *Thou shalt not commit adultery*. No compromise, no softening of the rules by circumstance. The Lord God had made the law and it was the duty of his believers to obey.

The kiss was brief and then Lydia slipped from Valleius' hands.

"We're being very foolish," she said breathlessly.

"How?" His voice was harsh.

She wished achingly that she had the courage to tell him that she could not break God's law, that no matter what her own desires might be, there was a law to follow and obey. But she knew she hadn't the courage to say that to this mocking man. She hadn't the courage to risk his anger. She would have to try to handle this with adroitness.

"My daughter's up in her room, awake and old enough to be aware of —of what you're suggesting."

"I could come back later," Valleius said.

"Ditus comes in very late, sometimes earlier, but sometimes not until almost morning. I've trained him to stop by my door before he goes to his room."

Valleius stared at her. "You're making that up."

"I'm not. It's true."

He looked at her for a long time and then shrugged. "So what am I going to do?"

"You have a lovely wife whose greatest desire is to please you, I know," Lydia suggested.

Valleius twisted his shoulders but said nothing. A man who likes variety, Lydia thought. I wonder if Erosa —but no, wasn't the general belief that only virgins could see into the future? Valleius was probably more careful of the girl's chastity than he would be of his own daughter's.

"I think, Valleius, that in spite of how you say you feel about me, and in spite of the fact that you are a man who is enormously attractive, this thing shouldn't go any farther. There's still another reason —even beyond your wife and my children."

"You must sit up nights gathering your defenses against me," Valleius said bitterly.

"No, listen. That day Erosa came to see me, she pretended to prophesy but she was only warning me. She as much as told me to stay away from you, to not even be friends with you."

"I don't believe you. She wouldn't dare."

"Ask Fulvia."

"Are you afraid of her then? I thought you were immune to soothsayers," Valleius taunted.

"If she found out you came here," Lydia said, "and I have no doubt she would find out —you know how slaves gossip —and it angered the demon who possessed her so that it cast her to the ground and killed her, would that be worth an hour's pleasure, Valleius?"

The man stared at her for a long time, and there was admiration as well as anger and frustration in his eyes.

"You're shrewd, little one," he admitted. "And what makes it worse, much worse, is that everything you've said has been logical. But you haven't seen the last of me. I suggest you keep in mind that I'm an opponent worthy of your steel. There may come a day when every argument you've presented can be destroyed."

"In the meantime, my friend," Lydia said with sudden intensity, "be a good husband to Fulvia."

"She's never had anything to complain about," Valleius retorted. "She does exactly what she pleases, and not every woman can say that. I haven't even objected to this foolish notion of joining the Jews at their worship. If I weren't convinced that it was utter nonsense, I'd forbid it. So it might be wise for you to reverse that admonition and tell Fulvia to be a good wife to *me*."

There was undoubtedly a note of warning in his voice, and Lydia noted it with respect. She stood up and extended her hand.

"Thank you for paying me the honor of your attention," she said carefully, aware as she always was, that to antagonize this man too much would be disaster for her. "I'm sorry I must be so —so unresponsive."

His hand holding hers, Valleius stared down into Lydia's face. "Given an opportunity," he said, "I'd make you responsive. Be sure of that. And have no doubt, little one, that I'll be looking for just such an opportunity."

What was there to say to him? She tried to smile and felt her mouth tremble.

"Good night, my sweet," he said and his lips brushed hers.

"Good night," she answered and marveled at the strength that kept her lips from clinging to his.

Lying awake in her bed, Lydia went over and over the scene in the atrium. She was shocked at herself for her physical response to the man. He was, after all, married to her best friend, and what's more, she had thought that Reuben's laws and admonitions were more strongly entrenched in her. Morality, she figured out slowly, is not something which is acquired as a gift at the moment of believing and then is forever after a firm possession of the believer. Morality is something one must struggle for every day.

There was a sound at her door.

"Mother?"

"Yes, my dear."

"Mother, I'm home."

But it didn't sound like Ditus' usual announcement. The confidence and satisfaction that usually filled his voice were gone.

"Is something wrong, Ditus?" Lydia asked, raising herself on one elbow. "Are you all right?"

"I'm —I'm a little upset, that's all."

"Do you want to talk about it? Is there anything I can do to help?"

Ditus moved into her room and set his hand lamp on the chest. He looked unusually tall in the drifting shadows of the small light.

"Clement's wife died," Ditus announced baldly and then stood awkwardly in the middle of the room.

"Oh, Ditus! Oh, the poor soul. Here, come and sit on the edge of my bed. What happened? Were you there?"

"Yes. Clement was called home; a soldier came to relieve him. I thought I might be able to help so I went along."

Lydia pulled her pillows so that she could sit upright against them and Ditus sat on the edge of the bed. His face was so distressed and his eyes so bleak that Lydia reached over to take his hand. The fact that he let her hold it indicated how great his pain must be.

"She was screaming," Ditus said. "Usually at night they could give her mandrake and she could get a few hours sleep. But lately it hadn't been helping much. They knew she was dying. They —" and his voice trailed away.

"I know, my dear," she said. "I'm sorry."

"You can't know," he cried. "The terrible way she

screamed."

"I heard a woman screaming once," Lydia said. She had almost said "I heard *her* screaming once." It was getting harder and harder to keep Ditus from knowing of her meeting with Clement. "One morning coming past the garrison. So I can imagine what it was like."

"Why is life like that?" Ditus demanded. "Why are people allowed to die like she did, screaming and writhing and begging Clement to kill her."

Lydia's heart twisted. How unbearable it must have been for the man, how dreadful for the boy who saw it all.

"I don't know," she said simply. "I just don't know."

"I shouldn't have gone," Ditus went on, acting as though he hardly heard her, as though his question had been mere rhetoric. "I didn't know what to do or what to say. I was only in the way."

"No, I'm sure not. If Clement is your friend as you say, then he would have felt your caring. I'm sure he would."

"Clement didn't even see me. He just held her while she begged him to use his knife on her. He just—held her. But when it was over—when she died—he put his head down and cried. Like a child."

Lydia chose her words carefully. "Ditus, there's no shame in weeping. Clement must have loved her. I don't know how he kept from crying sooner."

The boy stared at his mother. "I don't either," he whispered. "But he's—he's stronger than anyone I know. He never lets his feelings show. Never. That's why—"

"That's why you were so shocked when he cried," Lydia finished for him. "If Clement is all you say he is, I imagine he'll thank you for forgetting what you've seen tonight."

Ditus glanced away from her and then back. "Yes, you're right," he mumbled. "I—I'll just have to act like he acts. As though nothing mattered. As though nothing mattered at all."

Lydia nodded her agreement and briefly laid the boy's hand against her cheek. "Now go to bed, my son. Try to sleep. The horror will go away; believe me, it will."

"Thank you," Ditus said, and for the first time in years, he bent forward and kissed his mother's cheek. "Good night."

"Good night, Ditus. May the Lord bless you and keep you."

He moved away from her blessing nervously, as he would move away if threatened by a wasp. He picked up his lamp and turned away.

"Thanks again," he said and left her room.

She adjusted her pillows and lay down slowly. Her fingers came up and touched the spot where Ditus had kissed her. She had almost forgotten the heat of Valleius' mouth, and her own affairs dimmed in the light of what had happened to Ditus. There is no way, Lydia thought soberly, to protect our children from the ugly things in life. No way to keep them safe. Even my prayers don't shield Ditus from grief or shelter him from cruelty.

part two

And . . . Lydia . . . was listening, and the Lord opened her heart to respond to the things spoken by Paul.

And when she and her household had been baptized, she urged us, saying, "If you had judged me to be faithful to the Lord, come into my house and stay." And she prevailed upon us.

Acts 16:14b, 15

12

The winter rains were over. Sunshine flooded the early Sabbath morning as Lydia, Fulvia, and Minta walked along the path that led from the Via Ignatia toward the meeting place on the banks of the Gangites River. It was good to be outside again, although even in the cramped quarters of Miriam's house, the Sabbath meetings had continued to enrich Lydia's life.

As a matter of fact, the weekly meetings had been rewarding in several ways. Not only had her knowledge of God's laws and promises grown, but her sense of oppression resulting from being confined to the shop during the rainy season had been lightened. The early excitement of working and confirming her own abilities had diminished during the wet weather, and she had found some days tedious and limiting.

Lydia realized that some women —those who did not think her bold and unfeminine —looked on her as liberated because she ran her business competently and apparently without the help of men. But *she* knew how confining the responsibilities of the shop were. If Ditus were only older and more responsible, if she were only certain that the boy could be trusted to conduct the work as she believed it ought to be conducted, she'd be tempted to turn the whole thing over to him.

Her sense of responsibility was even heavier since Reuben was no longer working every day. When the winter rains turned the shop damp and chilly in spite of the two braziers that were kept burning at all times, the old man had complained of stiffness and pain. At last, Lydia had suggested that he work only on the days he really felt well enough to come out, and these proved to be rare. She knew he deserved total retirement, but she couldn't bear to give him up. She loved him as a father, and when he could, he still taught her and Fulvia the truths about God. He read the scrolls in his scratchy sing-song that etched the words into the deepest part of Lydia's being. Daily, her love for the old man and the Scripture he read increased.

She didn't understand the more complicated parts of the Law. She made no attempt to run her household along the lines that, for example, Miriam ran hers, but Reuben seemed to think that if she believed, if she memorized the words of the Lord, if she accepted the covenant with faith, she would be doing enough. He kept reminding her that he was *not* a Pharisee, a rigid observer of the Law, but he certainly claimed for himself a place in the covenant that the Lord had made with his chosen people.

Well, Lydia reflected, the important things were that Reuben had led her to his God and that both Fulvia and Minta shared the joy and reassurance that was hers. If her own faith sometimes seemed to falter, at least she had been given some strength and some courage.

"Everybody's here," Minta announced, breaking into Lydia's reverie.

"Yes, I see he is," Lydia responded and the look she shot her daughter was gently mocking.

Minta blushed but her shining eyes followed every movement David made as he set up and lit the lamp and placed the box in its proper place. That Minta was deeply attracted to the boy Lydia knew, and one of the questions that plagued her at night when she was too tense to sleep was what was to be done about it. She honestly was not sure what she'd do if Miriam came to her one day with a suggestion that a marriage be arranged between the two young people. David was only a cobbler, running a tiny shop that had been his father's. Minta would never again have the luxuries that she had known since birth.

But, to balance that, David was deeply rooted in the faith, and the girl would never have to know spiritual poverty. Fulvia declared herself totally unable to advise, and there was no one else to whom Lydia could turn. As a result, she tried not to think of it any more than she had to.

"Don't let your heart shine too brightly in your eyes," she whispered softly, squeezing Minta's hand affectionately.

Minta smiled but did not lower her eyes. She's candid and honest, Lydia thought, and terribly vulnerable.

The people seated themselves. When silence had fallen, David stood and started to open the scroll.

"The reading today is from Isaiah," he announced. "We will hear the promise of God."

Fulvia nudged Lydia sharply, and Lydia, jerked out of her anticipation of the reading, looked in the direction Fulvia's eyes directed her to look. To her astonishment, she saw four men coming toward them from the direction of Philippi. They were obviously not Roman because they wore the same kind of simple robe that Reuben and the other Jews wore. Their heads were covered, and they walked with a purpose that could only suggest that they had come seeking this small band of people.

David stopped speaking and stood, openmouthed, watching the men approach. Reuben and the others also stared without movement. No one from the garrison or the town of Philippi had ever objected to this weekly gathering, although Reuben had told of persecution in other cities and states, so it seemed unlikely that these strangers would cause trouble. Nevertheless, caution stamped itself on every watching face.

The four men stopped a few feet away, and the shortest of them stepped slightly forward.

"This is a synagogue meeting of Jews?"

Reuben made a gesture which indicated the lamp and the box. "What else then?"

The stranger inclined his head. "My name is Paul, Paul of Tarsus. This is Luke, this Timothy, and this Silas," he went on, indicating the other men who were with him. "We are traveling from Jerusalem and have recently arrived in Philippi. When we looked for a place of worship as the Sabbath approached, we were told that there were very few Jews in the city."

"Just us," Reuben agreed. "And not every person here is a Jew."

"No?" Paul's eyebrows rose.

"A few residents of the city have learned from us about the Lord God of Israel."

Paul smiled and glanced at his companions with a triumphant look. "There may be fertile soil here," Paul murmured to one of them. "How does it seem to you, Silas?"

The man nodded without speaking.

"So we've sought you out," Paul said, "and we're sorry to be late. Please don't let us interrupt any further. I believe we were about to hear the reading of the Scripture."

"If you'll be seated," Reuben urged, and the visitors sat down with the other men.

"As I started to say," David began, and his voice squeaked from nervousness. Minta winced with pity. "I will read the promise of the Lord from the prophet Isaiah, the promise that has been the hope of Jews for centuries."

Lydia could not help noticing that Paul's eyes, which had been cast down toward the ground before David spoke, were suddenly intent with such fervor that she found it uncomfortable to look at him.

"Hear the promise of the Lord God of Israel," David began. Gradually, his voice slowed and steadied, becoming the proper vehicle for the lovely words.

"The people that walked in darkness have seen a great light; they that dwell in the land of the shadow of death, upon them hath the light shined.

"Thou hast multiplied the nation, and not increased the joy; they joy before thee according to the joy in harvest, and as men rejoice when they divide the spoil."

David seemed to forget the visitors as he continued to read, and Lydia, like the others, heard only the boy's voice.

"For unto us a child is born, unto us a son is given; and the government shall be upon his shoulder: and his name shall be called Wonderful, Counsellor, The mighty God, The everlasting Father, The Prince of Peace.

"Of the increase of his government and peace there shall be no end, upon the throne of David, and upon his kingdom, to order it, and to establish it with judgment and with justice from henceforth even for ever. The zeal of the Lord of hosts will perform this."

In total silence, David rewound the scroll and sat down. Of all the words of Scripture which Lydia had read or heard, these, she had learned, were those which stirred the people most. It was as though each time the words were heard, the people's hope was lifted to a new height.

Reuben turned with courtesy to the strangers. "Would one of you care to speak?"

Paul nodded and leaned slightly forward. He began to speak in a low but strangely persuasive voice. "The Lord God *caused* those words to be chosen for today's reading, because he has sent me here to tell you the good news that this prophecy has been fulfilled. The coming of the Messiah which Isaiah foretold has been accomplished in this time."

The sound of indrawn breath hissed in Lydia's ears. She looked from face to face, expecting to see only joy. Wasn't this what they had longed to hear for centuries? But instead, she saw incredulity, shock, and even anger.

"What do you mean?" Reuben's voice was shaking.

"I mean the Messiah has been born, has lived among us. He has returned to God, but his Spirit moves here in this place. He was killed by Roman soldiers but he triumphed even over death."

The words were incredible to Lydia. No one had ever defeated death; it was the ultimate victor in every life. God might enrich this existence, but when it ended, everything ended.

"Let me tell you," Paul begged, meeting the resisting and disbelieving faces with a steady, burning stare. "Please let me tell you how it was with me, how the truth was given to me. Will you let me speak?"

There was some muttering, but Reuben raised his hand for silence.

"Our guest will be heard," he said sharply. It took a few minutes for an uneasy silence to settle over the people, but finally it was quiet enough for Paul to begin.

Paul was not an attractive man, Lydia realized. His skin was darkened and dried from the sun, and his hands were the calloused, hardened hands of a laborer. A high, domed forehead bulged over a narrow, aesthetic face. But his eyes were remarkable. They were blue, which in itself was remarkable in a land where most people had dark eyes. But the intensity that blazed in them was more startling than the color. If she looked long enough at those eyes, Lydia thought, she would lose herself and never again be able to recapture the essence of what she was at this moment. It was a disturbing thought, but she was unable to tear her own eyes away.

"I, Paul," the little man began.

From the first words, Lydia was so caught up by the message Paul preached that it was as though she were experiencing the events he described with her own body. She, too, sat at Gamaliel's feet; she, too, ignored that teacher's injuctions against intolerance; she, too, persecuted the followers of the young Nazarene. Breathless and dry mouthed, she winced from the pain of the stones that thudded against Stephen's flesh. Her arms felt the weight and texture of the woolen robes that had been held in Paul's arms. She felt her mind reeling in astonishment as Stephen died, forgiving those who killed him.

The blinding light on the road to Damascus struck into Lydia's eyes with devastation and she, like Paul, knelt at the sound of the voice of the risen Lord. She was trembling with a strange combination of exhaustion and exhileration when Paul finished his account of his own experiences. The man's voice and choice of words wove a compulsion that permitted her no possible escape back into the unknowing of yesterday.

With a short word of apology for interrupting his message, Paul got laboriously to his feet. Luke was there in an instant, assisting him, massaging his back with gentle hands. It was only then that Lydia saw the deforming hump which forced one shoulder higher than the other and pushed Paul's head forward. He had appeared to be leaning forward with intensity. Now she saw he was pushed into the posture of intensity by his deformity.

"Forgive me," Paul said. "I bear this thorn in the flesh and tire too easily. If you'll sing for a minute, I'll rest and then return to tell you the remainder."

While he walked to the edge of the river, the people sang obediently, their resistance broken for the moment by the man's persuasion. Reuben's face was luminous with excitement, David was staring after Paul as though he were looking at some divine being, and Minta's face was a reflection of David's.

Lydia sat in a daze. Something had happened to her while Paul talked, something she did not even try to understand. So she merely waited while her lips formed the words of the hymn, waited impatiently for Paul to come back to tell the rest of his story.

13

"What do you think?"

Fulvia's sudden whisper was a shock. Lydia had forgotten everyone but Paul.

"I've never heard anyone like this," Lydia admitted. "He's not an incredible speaker. But what he has to say is the most—well, exciting is the only word I can think of—most exciting thing I ever heard."

"I don't know," Fulvia murmured doubtfully. "He's different from Reuben. I've been so impressed by the intellectual logic of these Jews. This Paul is—is—"

"On fire," Lydia supplied. "I can't imagine what it must be like. I believe in God with my mind, but oh! to be like that, blazing inside—"

"Shh! Here he comes," Fulvia whispered.

Paul rejoined the group and lowered himself to the ground again. He looked around the circle of faces intently.

"I've told you what happened to me," he said. "You need to know that to understand with what authority I speak. But now I bring you the good news of Jesus Christ and how he can bring his mercy and love and peace to *you*."

Once more, Lydia was swept out of herself by the power of Paul's words. She listened to the sayings of Jesus, was stunned by his miracles, cringed under the whips of his tormentors, agonized as he hung on the cross and exulted at his appearance beside the empty tomb.

"It was a woman who saw him first," Paul said, and for the first time he looked directly at Lydia. "A woman who spoke to him and brought the news of his resurrection."

And Lydia believed. There was no room in her for doubt or misgiving. When Paul told of the wind and fire that had touched the believers that day in Jerusalem, when he promised that the same power was there for the asking, she trembled with eagerness and desire.

"How do I get this power?" she begged. Immediately, she was sharply aware of the disapproval around her. Women never spoke out in meetings, but she could not stop the words.

Fortunately, David breathed the same question, so Paul could turn to the boy.

"You have only to believe and be baptized."

Baptism was not a practice of this group, although everyone knew what it was. The river was there beside them, and eagerly they hurried to the water.

Lydia was aware of no one and nothing but her own need for this gift which Paul had promised. She was not even thinking of Minta. Eagerly she pushed through the crowd until she reached the edge of the water. She dropped her stola and stood waiting in her simple tunic.

Silas and Luke waded out into the river, and she saw the involuntary shudder that shook them as the cold water came up to their waist; but she was sure that they hardly felt the chill. They must be burning with the same invisible fire that blazed in Paul as he stood on the bank, his hands raised in blessing.

It was young Timothy who took her arm to lead her out to Silas and Luke.

"Don't be afraid," Timothy said softly. "They will lower you into the water, and then they will lift you out. There's nothing to be afraid of."

Afraid? She stared at him in astonishment. It had never occurred to her that she might feel any fear.

As Silas and Luke steadied her between them, Paul began his catechism.

"Do you believe in God?"

"Yes, oh, yes," Lydia cried.

"Do you accept what you have heard about Jesus the Christ?"

"Yes."

"Do you believe that God's Holy Spirit can move in your life?"

"I do believe," she answered.

"Then let this act be a death of your old life, and a resurrection to a new faith."

Paul's voice rang out with joy. "In the name of Jesus —"

The waters closed over her. But it was not Silas' hands which held her and kept her from sinking into the darkness of a watery death. She was lifted up and buoyed up by the hands of God. She knew it as surely as she knew that the sun would rise each new morning.

Emerging from the water, she felt again the humanness of Silas' and Luke's hands holding her and steadying her.

"Go, my daughter," Paul said, and for an instant his cool, aesthetic face was warm with love and joy. "Go and do the will of God in the spirit of Jesus Christ."

She walked out of the water, oblivious to everything except the happiness that filled her. For a minute she stood dazzled and dazed, and then she bent to pick up her stola. Its dry warmth was comforting in a plain, homely way that was oddly sweet after the touch of divinity.

She looked back toward the river in time to see Minta coming out of the water, her face glowing. Picking up the girl's dry stola, Lydia held out her arms, and Minta walked into her embrace.

"Oh, Mother," Minta said.

She was not even looking for or thinking about David, Lydia realized. She, too, had been touched by something unbearably beautiful.

Lydia only hugged her daughter tightly and then helped her drape the stola around her. She pushed the heavy, wet hair back from Minta's face and saw the tears mingled with river water.

"You're a blessing to me," Lydia said.

Minta only smiled and kissed her mother's cheek. There were, Lydia realized, no words that needed to be said.

Gradually, Lydia began to really look at the people around her and to become aware of who had accepted the baptism and who had not.

Reuben and David were among those whose clothes were wet, and the same radiance shone on the old face and the young face. But Lydia was grieved and surprised to discover that Fulvia stood, dry and aloof, at the edge of the group.

"Were you not convinced, my friend?" Lydia asked, going over to her.

Fulvia smiled wryly. "I thought you knew me well enough to realize that I'm rarely swayed by emotion alone. I want my mind to tell me what to do. And I don't know enough about this Jesus. Paul says he rose from the dead. Perhaps. But I want to know more. I want to know more of what he said while he was alive, what he did. I want to know why God found it necessary to create a *man* to represent Him. I've been deeply touched by the things I *know* about the Lord God Jehovah. I don't know enough about Jesus."

Lydia shook her head, feeling the weight of her wet hair. "I don't understand. It just seems so clear to me. But —there must be some way for you to learn what you need to know!"

Fulvia shrugged slightly. "I wonder how long they're staying," she said.

Lydia looked over to where Reuben and David were standing with Paul and his friends. Reuben was shaking his head with regret. Moving closer, she heard the old man say, "I wish I could offer you my home. But there's only one room for sleeping, a very small one at that, and another one for eating and sitting. There just wouldn't be room."

"Well, perhaps we should go back to Neapolis," Luke said. "I have old friends and even some family near there."

But Paul spoke stubbornly. "I want to stay in Philippi. I think I'm supposed to stay here. The Lord will provide a place to sleep."

It didn't occur to Lydia to consult Minta or to seek advice from Fulvia or Reuben. She simply spoke from her heart.

"Come to my house to stay. I have plenty of room. Not large rooms, perhaps, but there are several small ones off the atrium which we aren't using. You're more than welcome to them."

Reuben frowned. "Is such an invitation proper from a widow, Lydia?"

"I never even thought of that," Lydia admitted. "I only heard Paul say that he wanted to stay here in Philippi, and I have enough room."

Paul spoke quickly. "Have you children? Slaves?"

"My daughter was baptized here today, sir. My son is almost a man; his seventeenth birthday will be in a short time. He'll confirm my invitation. And, yes, I have slaves."

Automatically, her gaze went toward the place where several of the slaves always waited for her. To her astonishment, she saw that their clothes and hair were wet. "Did you baptize them?" she said in astonishment. "But they're only slaves."

"In the sight of God, everyone is the same," Paul said sternly. "Male and female, free man and slave."

"It will take some thinking," Lydia confessed, "to adjust to the idea that my slaves *believe*. It never occurred to me to share my God with them."

"But we've been listening, Mistress," Pyrus, the nearest slave, said. "Each week we've been listening."

"So you see, sir," Lydia said, turning back to Paul, "I *do* have slaves, and they have received your baptism. Surely, this would make it proper for you to come to my home."

"And a son, you say? A son who is nearly a man?"

"Yes, a son." She caught sight of Fulvia, standing alone and waiting. Fulvia *needed* instruction from these men. "Oh, please, sir," Lydia pleaded with sudden intensity. "I've been deeply moved by what you've said, but I must hear more. If you count me worthy, come to my home."

Paul looked at the three men who had come with him. "What do you think?"

"The lady may be risking the possibility of gossip," said Silas. He was a large man, younger than Paul. His hair and beard were dark, but his eyes were a curious light color, almost gray.

Lydia drew herself erect. "I do not anticipate gossip. I'm a woman of honor, sir."

It was Luke who spoke soothingly. "Of course. I say we should accept her invitation and be grateful. What do you say, Timothy?"

The youngest of the men looked at Lydia shyly. "I should like very much to stay in a house again. It will seem a luxury after some of the places we've stayed."

Lydia smiled at the boy. He couldn't be much more than twenty, she thought, and he probably needed a mother's care.

"Then it's agreed," Paul said. "We're grateful. Very grateful indeed. We'll have to go to the inn to settle our account and get our few belongings."

"I'll leave my slave, Pyrus, here to guide you," Lydia said. "I'll go on ahead with my daughter and my friend and get things ready."

Reuben spoke at last. "At least this means that you'll stay in Philippi, sir," he said to Paul. "You'll forgive me for being so cautious about Lydia? She's like a daughter to me."

Lydia felt the sudden stinging of tears. It was the first time that Reuben had expressed in words the feeling she had been sure he possessed.

Impulsively, she reached over and touched Reuben's hand. "Thank you," she whispered. "I don't know how I would have survived these past months without you. And now today—" She stopped, incapable of further words. Feeling tears on her cheeks, she only smiled and shook her head lightly. She turned away to start the walk back to Philippi with Minta and Fulvia.

"They're staying with you?" Fulvia asked.

"Yes. I know they'll talk to you, teach you what you want to know. I did it mostly for you."

When Fulvia didn't answer for a long time, Lydia looked at her anxiously. "Are you angry? I want you to know the utter joy that was mine when I was baptized. That's all."

"I know," was all Fulvia answered.

They were all quiet then, even Minta. Lydia let her thoughts go back to that moment when it had seemed as though God had actually touched her. Surely there must be some visible sign of that instant of holiness. She looked around at the grass and trees, the dusty path and the flawlessly blue sky that curved over their heads like an inverted bowl of precious azure glass. How could it all be unchanged? She felt as though the entire world should be different because of what had happened to her.

The machicolated wall of Philippi loomed in front of them, and still in silence, the women walked through the arched stone gate.

"There's Valleius," Fulvia said abruptly.

"Will he be angry, do you think?" Lydia asked, brought back to common things with a jolt.

"Why should he? He knows where I've been." But there was an uneasy look on Fulvia's face. "I see he has Erosa with him. I suppose she's been prophesying; see how contented he looks? Like a cat full of cream."

At that instant Valleius caught sight of them. "My dear," he said coming up to them. "I was beginning to think you were never coming back. You've never been at the river so long before."

"It was—a special meeting," Fulvia said vaguely.

When Valleius glanced at Lydia his eyes stretched wide with amazement. "What happened to you?" he asked. "Your hair is wet, your clothes are wet. Was there an accident?"

Lydia looked uncertainly at him. "No, not an accident," she began. "It was—was—" At that instant she caught sight of Paul and the others coming through the arch.

"It was a religious ceremony," she said, acutely anxious to get away before Paul and Valleius would meet. "I must hurry home; if you'll forgive me, I'm chilled in spite of the sun."

"A religious ceremony?" Valleius said smoothly. "But you're dry, my dear," he added to Fulvia. "I thought you two shared every belief."

"Not every one," Lydia said tartly. "Neither of us tells the other what to do or think."

"Even when we may want to," Fulvia agreed, and there was something about her tone of voice that caught Lydia's attention. Was Fulvia angry, irritated, disappointed, or what? She couldn't take time to think about it now. She had to get away before Paul came.

Erosa, who had been moving around them in circles, suddenly spied the group of strangers coming along the street. She ran toward them with a swiftness that even Valleius' sharp command, "Erosa, come back here!" could not halt.

She looked intently at Paul and his friends, and Lydia could see the rigid set of the girl's shoulders and the trembling of her hands.

"These men are servants of the Most High God. They will proclaim the way of salvation," Erosa cried.

Paul stared at the girl wearily. "Doesn't she belong to anyone?" he asked.

"She belongs to me," Valleius announced, his voice hard with anger.

Paul looked at the tall Roman and then bent his head in a gesture of acknowledgment. "As you say," he murmured indifferently and then, glancing at Lydia, "We'll see you at your house then, Mistress Lydia?"

"At my house," Lydia agreed. Catching Minta's hand, she almost ran down the street, away from Valleius' anger and his slave's madness and the wholly incomprehensible coolness of Fulvia, whose thoughts, Lydia had believed, would always match her own.

14

"There!" Lydia said to herself as she stepped back to admire the vase of orange blossoms she had placed on the table in the atrium. There was so brief a time before Paul and his followers would arrive—probably as soon as sundown marked the end of the Sabbath—that she had been able to do very little in preparation for them. Fortunately, Kora kept everything so clean that Lydia had only needed to have a house slave air out the little sleeping rooms off the atrium.

I hope everything will be all right, Lydia thought, looking around with an anxious frown. She glanced down at her fresh stola, carefully draped and delicately perfumed. Her hair was not as perfect as usual, she knew, because of this morning's wetting. Kora had done her best, and for once, Lydia was grateful for the natural curl that dried into ringlets.

It was strange to be preparing for guests. While Aurelius lived, having guests had been a common occurrence. But life had been very different during the year since Aurelius' death.

A year. Lydia stood very still, looking down at the mosaic on the floor, remembering how she had paced around and around it in her early agony. It didn't seem possible that almost a whole year had gone by, in spite of the varied and drastic changes that had occurred in her life.

Not all the changes were bad, she reflected honestly. The hours of learning spent with Reuben had been enriching beyond anything she had ever known. She had learned so much that it sometimes astonished her to see how her ideas had changed. Her old belief was that honesty and loyalty were admirable because the family and the state functioned better if these virtues were practiced. It had not been easy to accept a belief that, if one were dishonest or unchaste, one had sinned in the eyes of God. But certainly the growth had occurred in her, thanks to Reuben's teaching.

There had been other good things, too, during this year, she knew. Fulvia's friendship, Minta's closeness, the satisfaction of knowing that the business was going well—all these were sources of satisfaction to her.

There had been problems as well as accomplishments, she thought soberly, still standing motionless in the atrium, allowing her mind to recall the past months. Her handling of the business hadn't *always* been wise. Ditus was often surly and uncooperative, and there was the nagging worry of his coming-of-age ceremony, which should happen in only a few weeks. She hadn't even discussed it with Ditus because she simply hadn't made up her mind how to handle it.

Although she had made and discarded a dozen possible plans, she had developed no ready solution to the problem of who would take Aurelius' place in the ceremony, nor to the question of what she wanted to do about turning at least part of the management of the business over to Ditus on that day.

But of all her problems, the greatest was that she was still worried about Valleius. For weeks and weeks at a time, he would let her alone. Then he would find an excuse to see her again. So far, she had held him at arm's length, although her excuses were beginning to wear thin. He had made more than one remark about the fact that things would be different when a year had passed. Well, now a year had gone by. What was she going to do? How could she possibly explain to him that what he was proposing was a sin? She doubted very much that he had any conception of what sin was. He might concede that an affair would be dangerous or even unwise, but he would not know why she felt as she did.

In her most honest moments, Lydia knew that if she were exactly as she had been a year ago, Valleius might not be pursuing in vain. She had been lonely, very lonely, and Valleius could be almost frighteningly persuasive. If it had not been for Reuben's God—for *her* God. . . . She suddenly remembered Erosa shouting at Paul and the look of weary distaste on Paul's face. I'll have to ask Fulvia to try to keep the girl off the streets while Paul is in Philippi, she decided. It would be embarrassing and disturbing if the girl shrieked at him every time she saw him.

"I'm not sure that we have enough fresh mats for sleeping, my lady," Kora said, coming suddenly into the atrium. "There are two in very good shape, thick and filled with new straw. We have several others, but they're thin and matted down, and I'm not sure we can unsew and fill and sew them again, all before dark."

"It will just have to be done tomorrow," Lydia said. "Don't worry too much tonight. From what one of them said, they've been sleeping on the ground. I imagine anything would be better than that."

Kora nodded agreement and turned to go, but at the door, she hesitated. "May I ask a question, my lady?"

"Of course. Why not?"

"The two who accompanied you this morning—Pyrus and Talos—they've come home with wild tales. They claim they took part in some religious ceremony with you. Should I have them punished for lying?"

"They're not lying, Kora. They were baptized, as I was, but I really don't know what to say about it. Paul, the man who baptized them, seems to think it's permissible and fitting. I honestly haven't had time to think about it."

"I consider it presumptuous, my lady." Kora's face was prim and disapproving.

Lydia shrugged. "When Paul comes, he'll be able to clear everything up, I imagine."

"This Paul is a priest?" Kora dared to ask.

"A very special kind of priest. He travels around, telling the miraculous story of the Jewish Messiah. The men who are with him are friends, I think—or disciples. One of them, Luke, acts very concerned about Paul's physical condition. There was a look about him—Luke, I mean—that made me think of a physician. He may be one, for all I know."

"Then it's true that you have met these men only today?" Kora said, unable to hide the dismay on her face.

Lydia stared at her with cool disdain. "I believe you have work to do," she said stiffly.

Kora bowed slightly. "Your pardon, my lady. I'll see that the mats are at least aired and shaken."

I shouldn't have been so cold, Lydia thought, watching Kora walk away. But she has no right to ask questions. There's no one, really, who has the right to question what I do.

As if in refutation of her thought, Ditus came storming into the atrium to confront his mother.

"What's this that Minta's telling me?" he demanded. "What insane business has been going on? She's babbling hysterically about some sort of baptism and some man who was a god. Furthermore, four men are coming here, she says. Here, to *my* house."

"Don't you forget yourself, my son?"

"No, I don't. I've avoided actually quarreling with you for a long time, Mother, because I've pitied you, but —"

"Pitied?" Lydia exploded.

"Yes, pitied. Even though I believe with all my heart that

you've stolen my birthright, I've allowed it to go on because I knew you were grieving for my father. The work —*my* work —kept you busy and I thought it would comfort you."

Lydia stood staring at Ditus, shocked by his words.

"In a matter of weeks," Ditus went on, "I'll celebrate my seventeenth birthday. Do you know how many years I've looked forward to this —how my father used to tell me that I was peculiarly blessed because my birthday and the 'Coming of Age Day' were both on March 17? And you still treat me like a child."

"I do not," Lydia sputtered, unable to find words that would make her more articulate.

"You do —and an inferior child at that. We've hardly even discussed my coming of age. You act like you want to pretend it won't happen. All you do is talk about this god of yours, and you encourage Minta to act the same way."

"Ditus, listen —"

"I want to listen," he cried. "I want to hear what happened this morning to Minta. And to you. I want to know what foolishness prompted you to invite four strangers —all men —to the home of a widow."

"I thought you just said it was *your* home," Lydia rejoined bitterly.

"Our home, then," Ditus said. "Will you please, before I go mad, tell me what this is all about?"

Lydia turned to lead the way to one of the benches. As she walked past the marble-lined pool, she saw the reflection of the sky in the clear water. The sight brought back the memory of the way the surface of the river had shimmered only a few hours before. She thought of Paul's questions and her confident answers. But where was God's spirit when all she was conscious of was anger?

Oh, God, please! For Jesus' sake! The words were unspoken, but almost at once she felt a cooling sense of peace.

She sat on a bench and patted the place beside her.

"Here, sit here," she coaxed. "Please listen to me. Try to understand."

At the sound of her voice, low and clear instead of shrill and strident as it had been, Ditus shot an amazed glance at her.

"I'm listening," he said, and sat down, but his voice was uncertain.

"You know that Minta and I have come to believe in the Lord God Jehovah —that we believe he is not simply a great god among many gods, but the only God. No, don't interrupt. Let me talk. It's impossible to make you understand if you won't even listen. You must accept the fact that Minta and I *believe*. You may question what we believe —that's your prerogative —but you have no right to question the fact that we are persuaded that only the Lord is God."

"I suppose I can't tell you what to think," Ditus said, "even if I think it's silly."

"No, you can't. But to get back to this morning. Ever since Reuben's been teaching me, he has talked of the possible coming of a Messiah."

"A what?"

"A Messiah. A Savior. A fulfullment of the promise made by Jewish prophets for hundreds of years."

Ditus only shook his head, but Lydia went on persistently.

"The men who came to the meeting this morning —Paul, Silas, Timothy (you'd like him, Ditus, I know), and Luke —claim that this Messiah has come."

"Where? Here?"

"No, to the land of the Jews —Israel. He lived and taught and died there. He was—" her voice faltered because she could foresee Ditus' reaction—"was crucified by the Roman soldiers."

"Oh, Mother!" cried Ditus, disgust sharpening his voice.

"By all the gods! How can you believe anything good about a man who was killed as a criminal? You're an intelligent woman. What's the matter with you?"

"That isn't all." Somehow she stayed calm. "He—this Messiah—rose again from the dead. He was *seen*, Ditus. He—he overcame death."

The word that slipped from Ditus' lips was vulgar. He made no attempt to apologize for it as he jumped to his feet and paced about the room with agitation. "That's insane!" he stormed. "If these men who are coming here believe that rot, they're insane, too. I can't *believe* you'd be so taken in. Or let Minta be."

"I'm sorry," Lydia said helplessly. "It must be my fault that you feel like this. It was clear and logical and utterly believable when Paul told about it."

"Who *is* this Paul?"

"Paul of Tarsus. A Jew, but a man of greater persuasion than any I've ever known. I'm convinced he was sent from God."

"*I'm* convinced that you've been hypnotized by some clever charlatan. "We'll probably be murdered in our beds and everything of value in the house will be stolen," Ditus shot at her.

"Have you so little regard for my judgment?" Lydia asked.

"I'm afraid I do. You thought—oh, so innocently you thought—that you could be friends with Valleius Tatinius. If you were wiser in the ways of the world, you'd have known he's a man who thinks only of his own gratifications. Do you think I can't guess the problems you have with him?"

"If my memory is correct," Lydia said, "you once believed that I was encouraging him."

"I was hasty," Ditus said shortly. "I know better now.

But I'm sure you haven't solved your problem. *Our* problem. Because anything that affects the business, affects me, and you know he could create trouble."

She only looked at Ditus in astonishment. She had never dreamed he was so perceptive.

"I even question your leaning on Reuben," Ditus went on brutally. "He's an old man, a fanatic. I can't see where he can offer you any real strength."

"You don't know," Lydia insisted.

Ditus shrugged. "And Clement," he went on ruthlessly. "You probably thought of him as a boor, a common soldier."

Her heart jerked convulsively. "What do you know of — of —"

"Your meeting with Clement?" Ditus interjected. "Enough. I know that you met him at the Tatinius'. I know you had to see if I'd told you the truth. I'm not sure what Clement told you; he only laughed when I asked. But I'm sure you weren't impressed. He isn't the kind who would impress you.

"As a matter of fact," Lydia said slowly, deliberately, "I found that your Clement reminded me strongly of your father. Not in looks or words or even actions. In some other way — I don't know how to say it."

"In his strength," Ditus suggested. "In his goodness."

"I don't know," Lydia repeated. "I only know that I felt oddly comforted after I had talked to him."

Ditus had the grace to look embarrassed. "I just assumed since you never mentioned it to me, since you continued to object to my going to the garrison that you had — well, disapproved."

"And so I do," Lydia said promptly. "Not of your friend so much as of your insistence on going out at night and spending your time in activities that neither enlarge your mind or purify your soul."

"Oh, Mother! You sound so —so pious."

The word hurt. Lydia had used it often to dismiss people who had been critical and intolerant of everything but their own way of life. Now, Ditus was using it to describe her, and it wasn't true. It couldn't be true. She had discovered what life could be and ought to be, and was she to be condemned if she wanted to share her discovery?

Before she could respond to the criticism, Ditus spoke again. "We're getting away from what I came to talk to you about. These men you've invited to stay here. You don't even know them."

"Oh, Ditus, I *do*! Maybe not for any period of time — perhaps you're even right in assuming that I don't actually know their background. But I know positively that they're men of honor, that the story they told this morning was the greatest truth the world has ever known!"

Ditus shook his head wearily. "I can't believe this," he said. "I should have known when you started following Reuben around with stars in your eyes that you were losing touch with reality, with the things that really matter. How can you expect me to respect you —and it's respect you're always talking about —when you do foolish and possibly even dangerous things like inviting four total strangers to stay in our house? And you did it without even consulting or probably even thinking of consulting me."

His voice had risen until the last words were almost a shout.

Lydia had just opened her mouth to make an angry retort when a sound spun her around. Paul and his friends, led by Kora whose eyes were round with dismay, stood at the door.

"We have arrived, Mistress Lydia," Paul said in formal tones. "This is your son, then, the one you said would confirm your invitation to us?"

It was so obvious that they had heard Ditus' angry comments that Lydia could only stand speechless, feeling the heat of shame burn her face.

Ditus stood irresolute for a few seconds and then strode toward the door. "If you'll excuse me," he said brusquely, pushing past the four men. "I'm sure my mother will make you welcome."

In the silence that followed, the loud slam of the outside door formed an echo to the boy's incredible rudeness.

15

Although her cheeks were flaming with shame, Lydia faced Paul with her chin up.

"You are welcome in my home, sir," she announced in a clear, steady voice. "The rooms are not as comfortable as we had hoped to make them, but before another day has passed, they'll be more suitable."

She pointed to the small, cell-like rooms that opened off the atrium, three on each side. The men looked around with admiration.

"A beautiful house," Silas said. "The Lord doesn't usually lead us to such surroundings."

"But since he has," Paul said with conviction, "then it's quite obvious that he intends us to take advantage of it. With your permission, Mistress Lydia, we'll sleep and meditate here before we go into the city each day to preach the story of Christ."

"Whatever you want to do," Lydia agreed. "I hope you'll join us for meals."

"That would surely be an imposition," Luke began.

"Don't judge my hospitality by my son's actions," Lydia protested. "I want you to feel completely at home here."

Timothy smiled shyly. "Thank you," he said.

"Please choose your rooms and put your belongings there," Lydia said, "and then come into the peristyle and

153

rest. It's cool there, and I'm sure there's wine and fruit for your refreshment. I'll leave you now to get settled."

Minta was waiting for her in the peristyle, wearing a clean stola attractively draped, her hair freshly combed and her face radiant.

"Are they here, Mother?" she asked eagerly.

"Yes, they're here."

"You don't sound very happy about it. I thought you were really excited about their coming."

"Ditus was terribly rude to them. I'm humiliated that my hospitality has been made questionable."

"I think, Mistress Lydia, that you and I should talk about this son of yours."

Paul's voice was completely unexpected. Lydia jumped a little, but her face was carefully expressionless when she turned to face her guest.

"Your coming was a total surprise to him," she explained, because in spite of her own anger toward Ditus, she could not betray him to a stranger.

"And he was —may I say dutifully? —he was *dutifully* concerned for the safety of his mother with strangers in the house?" Paul asked.

"Yes—he—"

Minta interrupted. "I told him," she explained breathlessly, "I told him about the meeting this morning and about Jesus, and how you baptized us—and—"

Paul smiled at the girl but turned back to Lydia. "He's not a God-fearer, then, this son of yours? How is it that you are? And your daughter?"

Lydia sighed. "It's a long story, sir. Will you sit on the bench here and be comfortable? I'll try to tell you."

Minta offered him wine, but Paul waved it away and sat quietly, waiting for Lydia to begin. It wasn't casual relaxation that made him so still, Lydia realized. He was obviously disciplined so that he was in complete control of his body and mind. There would be no leniency in this man toward Ditus' rudeness, Lydia thought. Paul would probably expect everyone to have the same control over his life that he, Paul, had over his. Well, there was nothing to do but begin.

She told her story as succinctly as possible, starting with the agony of Aurelius' sudden death and ending with the meeting on the river bank a few hours before. Paul's eyes never left her face, but he made no comment.

"And then," she finished, not at all sure how to make herself clear, "you came and you told about a Messiah who had overcome death. It seemed to me the answer to everything."

Paul nodded, still without saying anything. Finally, he spoke quietly. "Your story is not a typical one. You've accepted God through faith, not an inherited tradition, so it makes your situation both easier and more difficult. Easier because you have already grasped the great principle that belief is the most important thing, but more difficult because you lack so much of the history and the Law."

"I know some," Lydia said. "Reuben's scrolls —we've studied them together. The first books of the Torah, most of Isaiah, some of the psalms of King David."

"You could read them?"

"They're written in Greek. I don't know where he got them. Reuben's past is —a mystery."

"The old man who was baptized? Yes, a strange man. He abides by the Law, apparently, but not rigidly. An enlightened man, I would say now. A heretic I would have said before I met the Lord Jesus."

"He taught me everything I know about God," Lydia said. "He taught me and my friend, Fulvia."

"A Roman lady?"

"Yes, her husband is a magistrate of Philippi. She and I

have shared much together—until this morning, that is. She—she wasn't baptized. She says she doesn't know enough about what Jesus said and did."

"You think you do though?" Paul's eyes were piercing under his gray eyebrows.

"Oh, no, sir, not nearly enough. But I didn't come to the baptism at the prompting of my mind, sir, but of my heart. I just felt—compelled!"

Paul nodded, evidently satisfied. "A good beginning," he murmured. "We plan to stay a while, long enough to establish a church in this town. A church made up of a group of men and women who will acknowledge Jesus as the Messiah and their Lord."

"There really aren't that many Jews in Philippi," Lydia began, "and only Fulvia and Minta and I are God-fearers."

"Anyone who will believe in the Lord Jesus Christ can be a part of the fellowship," Paul explained.

"I'm blessed," Lydia murmured, "to have you in my home."

"My friends are already resting," Paul said abruptly, "and I'm going to lie down, too. Will you excuse me?"

"Certainly. I'm sure you're tired."

Paul lifted his hands toward her and Minta as though he were offering a blessing, but his words were simple. "In the difficulties of my life, this stay in Philippi will be a blessing and a peaceful rest for my soul. I know it, thanks to you."

He disappeared toward the atrium.

Minta turned to her mother. "How could Ditus *not* like him?" she cried. "I just love him."

"Ditus doesn't know him," Lydia explained. "Of course, knowing Ditus, it's not going to be easy to get him to even listen to Paul. Ditus is—well, he's very angry at me. Until today, I hadn't known *how* angry." ·

"But Ditus always gets over being angry," Minta said in a comforting little voice. "He never stays angry with me."

"Then we'll just have to pray that he won't stay angry at *me*," Lydia rejoined, hoping her face showed more confidence than she felt in her heart.

Ditus was not home for dinner, nor was he there in the early evening when Lydia and Minta sat with their guests and listened to stories of Jesus. Fulvia was not there either, although Lydia had sent her a message announcing that Paul was going to talk and teach after dinner.

In spite of her concern over her son and her friend, Lydia was caught up in Paul's teaching. All the love and devotion she had felt toward God seemed sharpened and intensified by what she was learning. Because she had come to God with a fresh mind, uncluttered by old philosophies and prejudices, she was peculiarly open to the new concept of God which Jesus had taught, she discovered.

When the final goodnights were said and Lydia went to her own room, she was filled with a sensation of love and happiness that exceeded anything she had ever known. In that frame of mind, she felt only compassion and forgiveness toward Ditus, only concern for Fulvia. She was sure, as she drifted off to sleep, that all her worries were behind her.

She was still smiling in her sleep when Kora, a lamp in her shaking hand, came into Lydia's room, weeping.

"My lady, my lady," she cried, shaking Lydia by the shoulder. "Oh, come quickly. It's the young master. He's been hurt!"

Lydia came awake with the feeling that a cold hand was clutching her by the throat. "Ditus?" she said thickly. "You mean Ditus has been hurt —what —where?"

She never even thought of the male guests in the house. She simply flung back the cover on her bed and ran, wearing only her tunic which, ungirdled, fell almost to her ankles. Kora led the way toward the steps that led down to the hall and the outside door.

"What?" Lydia panted. "What is it? What happened?"

Kora's voice was as breathless as her mistress'. "I don't know," she confessed. "A man brought him. I think there was a fight."

"A fight? Ditus? Oh, no!" Lydia moaned.

Kora stopped so abruptly that Lydia nearly fell. "Here, my lady," she said and lowered her lamp.

At first Lydia could see nothing. Only a blur of white and crimson. Then her vision cleared, and she saw Ditus lying in a crumpled heap on the hall floor. His tunic was torn and bloody, and there was a gash across his forehead from which he had evidently bled profusely.

"Is there no one with him?" Lydia cried.

"A man brought him, carried him, my lady, but he said he had to get back. His name was Clement, he said."

"And he left my son here to bleed to death," Lydia said bitterly. "What kind of man is that?"

"A frightened man," Kora answered. "He said he's the jailer, my lady. If his prisoners would escape while he's gone, he'd be killed. You know the law. Even I know that."

"But look at Ditus. He could have—"

"He carried him home, my lady," Kora insisted. "He didn't leave him until he knew I was awake and had gone after you."

Lydia looked down at her unconscious son, and terror chilled her until she thought she would never be warm again. Ditus' face, in the uncertain light of the lamp, was pasty white where it was not smeared with blood.

"What shall we do?" Lydia wailed. "Get some water, Kora. Some cloths. Send one of the slaves for a doctor."

"If you'll permit me, mistress," said a quiet voice. "I'm a doctor. May I look at the boy?"

Lydia looked up to see Luke, with Timothy standing behind him.

"Oh, yes, please! I—he looks as though he were dead."

Luke put his ear on the boy's chest. After a silence, which

seemed to Lydia to stretch into infinity, Luke raised his head. "He's alive, but he seems to have lost a lot of blood. Can we get him someplace where he can be put on a bed? I'll need some water. Timothy, get my bag. Do you have a slave who can help me carry him?"

"Kora," Lydia cried, "get Pyrus. Hurry."

But the man was already there, aroused by the noise, and he and Luke carried Ditus to the small room where the boy slept.

"Now," Luke said. "If you'll all leave. All but the mother. Can you stand the sight of blood?" he asked.

Lydia replied stiffly. "I'm a mother, sir. I can stand anything."

She held Ditus' head while Luke cleaned the ugly head wound and pulled the edges together to sew them shut. Each time the curved needle bit into the flesh, she felt her own flesh cringing.

There were other bruises on the boy, one an angry, swollen mark on his back.

"He's been kicked," Luke said tersely. "That's a bad one. I hope no damage has been done."

Lydia felt tears slip down her face and was unable to stop them. Where was the beautiful serenity she had known when she fell asleep? Where was the God to whom she had given her love and adoration? Why had this terrible thing happened?

At some time during Luke's ministrations, Minta had crept into the room. White and sick looking but with her jaw set determinedly, she sat beside her mother.

"God will take care of him," she whispered. "I know he will, Mother."

Lydia swallowed the words that pushed up into her throat. It was almost impossible to keep from crying out, "Where was God when Ditus was attacked?" But, for Minta's sake, she refrained.

"How does he seem?" Lydia asked Luke.

The man's face was troubled. "He's been badly hurt and, as I said, he's lost a great deal of blood. I won't deceive you. He's in bad condition. Perhaps you'd like to call in another doctor."

"I've been watching you," Lydia said, forcing her voice to be calm. "You're obviously skilled and able to do anything that another doctor could do. But —what about medicine? Is there anything you need that you don't have with you?"

Luke shook his head. "I have healing ointment for the cuts, and later on, if we need it, I have sleep-producing drugs to stop pain. There's really nothing else that would help."

"But shouldn't he be waking up?" Lydia cried, panic sharpening her voice. "The bleeding is stopped now. He ought to be waking up."

"Yes," Luke agreed. "He ought to be. Unless there's bleeding I can't see. And if there is, there's nothing we can do."

"We can pray." Minta's voice was very clear. "Can't we pray?"

"I haven't been with Paul very long," Luke confessed. "I'm a new convert myself. But I've seen Paul and Silas perform something that seemed like miraculous healing. Do you think we ought to call them, Timothy?"

But Timothy was not there, and even as Luke looked around with a puzzled expression, the sound of men's voices was heard.

"There is trouble then?" Paul's voice came from the doorway. "How did you know about this, Luke, when I heard nothing until Timothy came shaking at me, telling me the young man was dying."

Before Luke could answer, Lydia cried out, "Oh, no, not dying. God wouldn't let that happen. Please, please, *do* something!"

Luke reached across to take Lydia's hand in his. "Don't lose heart yet. Timothy just spoke hastily."

But the look which he gave Paul was one of deep concern, and Lydia felt as though her own life was draining out of her body.

"What happened?" Paul asked, looking down at the boy.

"We don't know," Luke answered. "A fight, evidently. He's been badly hurt."

Suddenly Lydia was overwhelmed with fear. She realized how this must seem to Paul. A young man, who had been rude and insolent, going out without explanation and returning beaten and bloody. To someone who didn't know Ditus, the boy would appear a ruffian, a scoundrel. Certainly no one worthy of prayer.

"You may not think he deserves your prayers," she began hysterically.

Paul looked at her sternly. "Didn't you hear me today when I told how Jesus forgave the men who were crucifying him? Do you still think that the good which comes from God is *deserved*?"

"Oh, I don't know," she sobbed. "I only know that my son is dying."

It was Minta who turned to Paul with strength and dignity. "You are closer to the Lord than we are, sir. Will you pray for my brother? Will you heal him?"

"Only God can heal," Paul said. "But I'll pray, of course. Who knows what plans God may have for this boy?"

He leaned over the bed where Ditus lay and placed his hands on the bandaged head. At first he prayed in silence, and then his voice was lifted in a strange blend of adoration, praise, and pleading. Lydia, listening, felt an unexpected sensation of warmth, as though Paul's words were melting the coldness of her terror.

There was sudden silence and Paul stood, his hands still resting on Ditus, his head bent. Lydia looked fearfully at her son's face. Did the silence mean that Ditus was dead?

Instead, she saw color in her son's cheeks and lips.

"His heart is stronger," Luke said.

"The Lord be praised," Paul said simply. "I'll leave the boy to you, Luke, and to his mother and sister."

He turned to leave the room and Lydia ran toward him. "Oh, thank you, thank you," she cried, her voice ragged and torn.

"Don't thank me." Paul's voice was harsh. "Thank God through his son, Jesus Christ. If a miracle has been given to you, I was only a tool."

"Yes, sir," she whispered.

Paul raised his hand briefly in a gesture that could have been a blessing or a farewell, and then he and Silas disappeared.

"You, too," Luke said to Timothy. "I'll watch a while with the boy's mother. You get some rest."

"If you need me—" Timothy began.

"We'll call," Luke promised.

Lydia persuaded Minta to go to bed, too, and then she and Luke were alone with the wounded boy.

"I don't understand it," Luke said after some time had passed. "It's happened like this before. I'm not even positive it's the prayer—or Paul's presence. I only know that, after the prayer, the natural healing processes begin, and health is restored."

"I'm a new convert, too," Lydia admitted. "I don't know much about prayer and what it accomplishes. But I know, beyond any doubt, that without it, Ditus would have died."

Luke smiled wryly. "Now, all you have to do is to convince your son that a miracle has happened, eh?" he said.

They turned together to the bed and found Ditus watching them, his eyes lucid and aware.

16

"How did I get here?" Ditus asked. His voice was weak but clear.

"Oh, Ditus! Oh, thank God, you're awake." Lydia dropped to her knees beside the narrow bed and laid her hand against her son's forehead. "No fever," she murmured. "Oh, Ditus, you're awake." Her voice broke. If Ditus had died, what would she have done? She put her head down against his arm.

The boy moved restlessly. "How did I get here?" he asked again.

"Clement brought you. Or so Kora said. I didn't see him."

"Clement?"

"Yes. But, Ditus—listen! You've been healed miraculously," she cried.

There was disdain on the young face. "If there was any miracle," he said in a faint, cool voice, "it was that Clement risked his life to leave his post even for a few minutes."

Lydia opened her mouth to argue, but Luke's eyes seemed to be warning her not to pursue it. So she said instead, "What happened? Can you tell me what happened?"

"I was in a fight," Ditus said. "Can't you tell? And I obviously didn't give a very good accounting of myself." His voice seemed to gain strength with each word.

"A fight? Ditus, you've never fought. You've —"

"It's never been necessary before," Ditus said and turned his face away from her.

"What do you mean —necessary?"

But Ditus refused to answer, and the stubborn set of his mouth told her she would get no information from him now.

Luke stepped forward. "I'm a doctor, sir. I've been attending to your hurts. There's one very bad bruise on your back where you've evidently been kicked. May I see to it?"

Ditus sent a hard, level stare up into Luke's face and then turned obediently onto his side. But when Luke lifted the boy's tunic, his back was smooth and clear of bruises.

"It's gone," Lydia gasped. "Look. It's gone! It *was* a miracle!"

Luke said nothing, but his lips were pursed in a soundless whistle.

Ditus turned so easily from his side onto his back again that it was obvious there was no pain.

"No doubt you saw blood on my back —or mud from someone's shoe. Please don't prattle about miracles. I've had all I can stand tonight."

Luke smiled down at the boy. "If there was no miracle, then I'm a very fine doctor. So I'll accept your decision for now."

Ditus scowled. It was clear that he wanted to say something else, probably something rude or insulting. But his eyes were suddenly very heavy and he blinked like a child trying to fight sleep.

"Just rest now," Lydia coaxed. "Don't think about anything. We'll talk in the morning. For now, just sleep."

"Thank you," Ditus said in a blurred tone, but his eyes looked at both his mother and the doctor.

He may not want to be in debt to a stranger, Lydia thought, but he couldn't help it and at least he had the grace to be courteous. In just a second, Ditus was asleep.

"I'll bring my mat up here," Luke said to Lydia, "and stretch out on the floor. You go to bed. There's nothing more you can do. The boy will be all right."

Lydia looked down at her sleeping son and then up at Luke. "I don't know what to think," she confessed. "I *know* what his back looked like before Paul prayed. I just don't know what to *believe*."

"I don't know what to tell you," Luke said. "Paul's the one who would know. He's the greatest man I've ever met and he'll have an answer for whatever is troubling you."

"Perhaps not as gentle an answer as I want," Lydia suggested.

"Probably not. He's never claimed gentleness to be his prime virtue."

"Well—if you're sure Ditus will be all right?"

"Ditus will be fine, Mistress Lydia. Go to bed and sleep well, knowing that your son is in God's hands."

It took her a long time to get to sleep. She couldn't stop thinking about Ditus, first thanking God for his amazing recovery and then wondering why Ditus had been fighting. It just wasn't the sort of thing he would do. It had been necessary, he had said. And, oh, the bleakness in his eyes when he had said it. But why *necessary*?

Her thoughts came around again to the healing that had taken place in Ditus' bedroom. It had happened so simply, so quietly that even now she hesitated at the word "miracle." But she had *seen* the bruise, angry, purple, mottled. She had seen the waxy pallor in her son's face, the look of death.

"Oh, God," Lydia moaned softly, "help me understand. Help me to *know*. For the sake of your Son," she finished, remembering what Paul had said in his prayer.

It didn't seem to her that she had slept at all when Kora

came in to shake her shoulder again. "My lady," she whispered, "The man, Clement, is at the door. Will you come?"

Lydia threw back the cover. "Tell him to wait in the peristyle and then come back up to help me get ready. I don't want to detain him any longer than necessary. He's probably come directly from the garrison."

"Yes, my lady," Kora answered and ran to carry the message.

Hastily dressed and feeling less confident than usual because of the minimum care given to her hair and to the draping of her stola, Lydia hurried down to meet Clement.

"We'll bother my guests less if we talk in the peristyle," Lydia murmured to Kora as they went together down the steps.

Kora continued to tweak at her mistress' stola as she whispered back. "They're all awake, my lady, each in his own room. They are all kneeling."

"They're praying," Lydia explained.

Clement got up from the bench where he'd been sitting. To her consternation, she saw that he, too, had a battered look. One eye was badly swollen and an ugly bruise showed along his jaw.

"You were fighting, too," she gasped without even the courtesy of a greeting.

Clement grinned, but his eyes contained no humor. "Not really. I just interfered when I discovered what was going on. Three against one is hardly fair—especially when the one is down and being kicked."

Lydia winced at his words. "Thank you," she said. "Thank you for helping him—for saving his life, I think. For bringing him home."

Clement's head jerked up. "Please, don't say that out loud. If the head of the guards learns that I left my post—even for a minute—" He paused and then said grimly, "You know what would happen to me if a prisoner escaped."

"Yes, I know. That's why I'm so grateful. I—"

Clement interrupted brusquely. "How is he? I wasn't sure when I brought him home that he'd survive the night."

"I didn't think so myself," Lydia admitted. "But Luke—a guest in the house—is a doctor. What's more—" She stopped abruptly, knowing she could not tell this man about Ditus' healing. She couldn't bear to see the ridicule that would fill his face.

"Then he's all right?"

"He's going to be all right—when the cuts heal. Would you like to see him?"

"No, I'd prefer that he didn't know I came. He doesn't need *me* to check up on him."

Lydia recognized the faint criticism implied in the words, and her chin went up defiantly.

"As long as he's all right, I'll be going then," Clement said. "I've become very fond of the lad. I would have—well, I'm glad he's not as badly hurt as I thought."

"Could you tell me why he was fighting?" Lydia asked suddenly. "He won't."

"Then I'm sure he doesn't want me to," Clement replied promptly.

"But I want to know."

"Are you so sure that you do?"

"I certainly want to know what it is that would make my peaceful son get into a street brawl. And a serious enough brawl that his friends had to come to his rescue," Lydia declared. "Ditus has never fought before."

Clement looked squarely into her eyes. "He's never had to protect his mother's good name before, either," the man said in a gentle voice.

Lydia felt such a shock at his words that she thought she would fall where she stood.

"My good name?" she gasped. "There's never been a stain on my name—never—"

"There were several drunk soldiers," Clement explained. "Soldiers who had apparently heard that you were entertaining foreign male guests in your home. They were angry with Ditus because he had beaten them soundly at dice. They—they taunted him.''

There was a cold sickness in Lydia. ''Where would they have heard it?'' she stammered.

He answered her question with one of his own. ''It's true then?''

''They're religious men,'' Lydia explained. ''Jews like Reuben. The inn isn't suitable and I had a place for them to stay.''

''Well, you weren't raped and robbed the first night,'' Clement said baldly. ''So at least they aren't wholly villainous.''

''They're saintly men,'' Lydia cried. ''I explained that to Ditus.''

''Did you ask his opinion?'' Clement demanded.

''No—I—''

''You told me once I would think you were a foolish mother,'' Clement said. ''I can forgive the foolishness of concern, but I certainly find it hard to understand a woman who thinks only of herself, not of her son.''

Lydia stared at the man facing her. ''You have no right,'' she began.

''Ah, but I do,'' Clement interrupted. ''I'm his friend. My son and he are like brothers. I know how desperately the boy wants to become a man. And I know you won't let him.''

She opened her mouth to speak again but he held up his hand. ''No, don't contradict me. I know I'm right. I could wish you cared as much about your son as you do about your new religion and your fancy Roman friends.''

With that, he turned and limped rapidly out of the peristyle, into the hall, and in just a second, she heard the outside door closing quietly.

He was wrong, of course. He had to be wrong. She couldn't endure it if what he had said was true. Who could she talk to about it, she thought desperately. Minta's too young, and Fulvia—Fulvia hadn't even acknowledged her message. There was no one. No one. And then, like a flicker of flame in a dark night, she thought of Reuben. There's Reuben, she thought with a sob of relief. Maybe Reuben could help her. Maybe he could say the words that she needed so desperately to hear.

17

As soon as she had checked to see that Ditus was sleeping soundly, Lydia called Pyrus to come with her. They hurried across Philippi to the small house where Reuben lived. The old man was up, sitting in the sun, his hands loose and relaxed, his eyes half shut. At sight of Lydia, he hurried to bring her a stool. Then he sat facing her, listening quietly while she poured out the whole story.

"I would guess that it's Valleius who's been talking about your guests," Reuben said.

"Valleius?"

"He's probably very angry. You've held him at arm's length for a year, and in a matter of hours you've given Paul and his friends the run of your house."

"Reuben!" Her voice was high and indignant.

"Oh, I know. I know. Don't yell at me. I know what Paul is. I know what blessed news he brings —but don't judge me as typical of my fellow Jews. I'm certain most of them will be reluctant to believe Paul's message —probably will never believe it."

She was impatient. "I don't care about that. Oh, I do, of course. But not now. I care about Ditus and what Clement said about me. Am I really as selfish as he said?"

Reuben pursed his lips. "Why do you insist on being in complete charge of the business, Lydia?"

She drew her breath in sharply and he raised a silencing hand. "No, think about it a minute. Why do you?"

"Because the business is essential if we're to keep the house and slaves; because if Ditus and Minta are to have all the things Aurelius dreamed for them, we must continue to keep the business successful."

"But why *you*?"

She stared at him. "You understood in the beginning," she said in a low voice. "I thought *you* would still understand."

Reuben reached over quickly and took her hand. He had never really touched her before, and she clung to his dry old hand. "I *do* understand. I understand a great deal. I know that there are days when you're weary and wish you didn't have the responsibility. But there are more days when you are happy and proud doing what you're doing—showing the town of Philippi that a woman can be as successful as any man."

"I don't think it's only pride that—"

"Perhaps not *only* pride, but you would be far from honest if you didn't admit that you're proud of what you've done," Reuben said.

"Satisfied at least," Lydia conceded.

"So satisfied," Reuben said relentlessly, "that you haven't bothered to really look around you. I don't think you've noticed that Marin no longer gives orders. He takes them. Ditus has grown up a lot during this year."

"You think I should turn the business over to him?" She was incredulous.

"I can't even answer that. If you do and you're resentful and jealous, things will be as bad as they are now. Maybe worse. If you could be sure you really want to do what's best for Ditus—"

"Of course I do," she cried. "He's my son. I do want what's best for him. It's just—just that I have to be sure he's able to do what has to be done."

"And were you so sure that *you* were able to do what had to be done that first day you came to the shop?" Reuben asked.

Lydia's mind flew back to that time of pain and fear and indecision after Aurelius died. But it was because she knew so well the agony of uncertainty that she didn't want to go through it again. Why couldn't anyone understand that?

"Ditus will be seventeen in a few weeks," she announced abruptly, changing the subject. "I don't know how to handle it. I don't know whom to ask to act as his sponsor. Valleius would be the logical one, but I'm afraid he'd think I meant something by the invitation. And the ceremony — the paying tribute to Roman gods — I can't permit that. Ditus doesn't believe in the gods of course, but he'll want the traditional ceremony, I know."

"Have you discussed it with him?"

"No—I—I haven't had time."

Reuben frowned. "My guess is that Ditus thinks you don't even care."

"Ditus never thinks about anything but himself," she cried.

"Perhaps he needs help. After all, Ditus doesn't know about God in the way you do. Have you even told him about what Paul told us?"

"He laughed at me." Her voice sounded sullen even to herself.

"I expect we'll have to get used to a great deal more than having someone laugh at us," Reuben said somberly.

Lydia flushed. She had come to be comforted and strengthened, not scolded.

"I'll have to get home," she said stiffly. "My guests will be ready for breakfast, if they haven't already eaten. I told Kora what to fix for them, but I must hurry."

"Lydia, my dear," Reuben said slowly. "I know you

came to me because you're troubled, because you want someone to say that everything will be all right. But how do I know what will be?"

"Thank you anyway," she said and turned away dispiritedly.

"Just pray," Reuben advised.

"I am praying," Lydia said. "But it doesn't seem to help."

There was a sad look on his face, but she knew he wasn't to be blamed for the way the conversation had gone.

She stopped at her house only long enough to check on Ditus and to discover that Paul and his friends were already gone, and then she went on to the shop.

With neither Ditus nor Reuben there to help her, she was kept so busy that she had little time to worry. The morning raced by so swiftly that she was astonished to discover that the sun was high in the sky and the shops were closing for the noontime rest.

I'll go home to see if Ditus is still all right, Lydia thought, reaching to pull the shutters closed so she could lock them.

"Let me do that!" The voice was harsh and unfriendly. Lydia looked up, startled, into the face of Valleius.

"May I show you something, sir?" she stammered.

"Don't be a fool, Lydia. I wouldn't come at noon to buy. You know that."

"Then —what?"

"Let me close the shutter so we can talk without interruption," Valleius said, jerking at the wooden frame.

"No, please." She was breathless. "If we're going to stay here while we talk, it will be safe to leave the shutter open. There's more air."

He peered at her. "You mean you think it will be safer for you if the shutter is open so we're clearly visible from the street." His eyes were angry.

It was so exactly what she had been thinking that she was unable to contradict him with any conviction.

"It gets stuffy with the shutter closed," she said weakly.

"Then we'll let it get stuffy," Valleius said shortly.

"No, wait. Reuben might come —or Ditus if he's feeling better. It would be —most unbecoming to find us here and the shutters closed."

Valleius stood with his hand on the shutter, looking at Lydia. "Why are you so suddenly concerned about your reputation, my dear, when you were indifferent to it only yesterday?" he asked.

"I did nothing wrong," she cried. "Why do you —why does everyone —persist in thinking I've been immoral?"

"Not so much immoral as foolish."

Lydia tried to make her voice reasonable. "Valleius, listen to me. The men are religious men. The leader, Paul —if you'd only listen to him you'd know that he's totally dedicated to his beliefs. I'm safe with them in my house — completely safe."

"You wouldn't even let *me* stay for an evening."

"But you, sir," she said, "had made your —your position very clear. You didn't want to talk to me about spiritual things."

She dared to smile even while she felt a stab of disgust at herself for being coy when she should have been bluntly honest.

"Nor did I!" Valleius agreed. "But my patience is worn out, my girl. I'm through being shoved aside while you fawn on fanatic old Jews and men you don't even know. I'm finished!"

She deliberately misunderstood him. "You mean you'll stop this foolish pursual and be willing to be just my friend?"

"I said nothing of the sort. The foolish pursual, as you call it, may be ended for now, but I see no reason why we should be friends. I have little fondness for people who make sudden decisions and act on them without any intelligent thought."

She almost said, "But I *need* your friendship." Somehow, she bit the words back. Instead, she said in a cool, proud voice, "As you wish."

"As I wish!" Valleius came very close to her. "You know what I wish —or you'd know if you'd stop running around talking sentimental drivel about a god who was raised from the dead."

"Fulvia told you that?" she asked, hardly able to breathe from her sudden excitement at the idea that Fulvia might be interested in Paul's message after all.

"That's another thing! Fulvia will not be going with you to those stupid meetings. I have forbidden it! I won't put up with any more of this!"

His voice was so savage and his face so fierce that she shrank away from him. She had suspected once that Valleius could be cruel, but until this moment she had not known how cruel.

"You're afraid of me," he discovered. His expression was smug and gloating. "Good. I want it like that. I don't want you to forget me, Lydia. I want you to remember that I'm around."

He took her suddenly in his arms, and his mouth was ruthless on hers. She tried to be passive in his embrace, but there was such a feeling of sudden revulsion in her that she had to force herself to be still.

"You don't struggle?" Valleius said in a cold voice. "You don't cry out for help?"

Lydia felt her helpless tears on her face, but her mind was suddenly fixed on the promise Paul had made. The power—the presence—was here if she only believed.

I believe, she thought firmly. Oh, I do believe! And she was able to look into Valleius' face without cringing.

Valleius' eyes were the first to drop. "This has been a sorry business," he muttered. "I had such hopes."

"I'm sorry," she said, and miraculously her voice was gentle.

"Erosa was right," he said through clenched teeth. "She said that first night that you'd cause me trouble. But I thought she meant trouble I could handle."

"I'm sorry," she said again. "About Fulvia. Please, would you reconsider? Won't you let her be my friend?"

His eyes glittered, but his voice was smooth as oil. "If I have my way—and I generally do—she'll eventually be your enemy. She and half the good people of Philippi."

With that, he swung away from her and walked so swiftly down the street that his slave had to run to keep up with him.

Stunned and shaken, Lydia stood in the stoa. The strength she had received so suddenly dissolved just as suddenly into fear.

Lydia's mind was so filled with her own troubles that she had to force herself to be hospitable to her guests at dinner. Paul was quiet and preoccupied, but Timothy and Silas were talkative and friendly. Luke was frankly exhausted from the previous night, so he concentrated on eating and trying to stay awake.

"I've never known a woman who ran her own business," Timothy confessed to Lydia. "Oh, I've heard of it, of course, but I never knew one personally."

"Neither did I," Lydia admitted with a wide smile. "I'm what I am out of necessity. I can't really say it's what I want to do. At least, not all the time," she added when Ditus lifted his head attentively.

Paul spoke up suddenly. "My own trade is that of making tents. My supplies are following us and will come in a few days. I'd like to set up a place to work. Have you any ideas?"

"I thought you only preached," Lydia faltered.

"I earn my own keep," Paul said shortly. "I'm not a charity case."

For the first time, Ditus eyed the older man with something that might have been approval.

"I really don't know," Lydia began. "I don't know where you could work. Perhaps in the back of our storeroom."

"Not enough room," Ditus declared, entering the conversation for the first time. "A tentmaker has to have more space. There's that plot of ground down by the olive grove on the edge of town. Valleius owns it, but I'm sure he'd let you use it."

His eyes were on his mother's face. She felt her cheeks flushing under his steady gaze.

"Not Valleius," she murmured. "Can you think of someone else to ask?"

"I?" Ditus said, a touch of mockery in his tone. "*I* think of someone?"

"Yes, you," she said steadily as though there were no one else at the table except her son and herself.

Ditus looked at her for a minute and then turned to Paul. "I'll investigate the situation for you tomorrow, sir."

Paul glanced sharply at the boy. "I hardly expected assistance from you," he said bluntly.

"I had a little sense knocked into me last night," Ditus said coolly.

"But you've recovered completely?" Paul asked. "What of the bruise on your back?"

Ditus' eyes darted rapidly from Paul to Luke to his mother. "There wasn't any bruise on my back," he said a little too loudly.

"No?" Paul said. "Luke's eyes deceived him in the dim light, then." He turned abruptly to Lydia. "Do you remember that girl who rushed at us at the gate yesterday? The one who was shrieking about us being the messengers of God?"

"Yes," Lydia said and felt her heart plunge sharply.

"She was doing the same thing today. Yelling and bleating like a silly sheep. Do you know her owner?"

"I know him," Lydia said evenly.

"Would you ask him to keep her home, locked up if necessary? She ruins my train of thought and distracts people when they ought to be listening most seriously."

"I don't think I can," Lydia said slowly and saw Ditus' eyes widen. "I—he—well, we're not friendly. I'm afraid he'd take it badly from me."

"I think we should talk about this, Mother," Ditus said in a hard, sharp voice. "Could we talk later?"

Lydia looked at Paul. He shrugged. "If you'll forgive us, Mistress Lydia, we'll retire early. This has been a difficult day. Luke is exhausted from staying up all night with your *healthy* son —" his eyes were sardonic as they touched on Ditus' face. "Silas and Timothy have both suggested a long night's rest. Could the teaching you've asked for wait until tomorrow?"

"Of course," Lydia said. "It's all for the best. It will give me time to talk to my son."

The most amazing sense of relief came over her as she said the words. She had thought herself alone, with no one to talk to, no one to understand. And here, all the time, she had Ditus. "You see," she said rather childishly to Paul, "you see I need very much to get some advice from Ditus."

Paul merely nodded politely, but Ditus' eyes began to shine as though a flame had been lit in their dark depths.

18

"Now," Ditus said after everyone else had retired and he and Lydia were sitting in the small office-like room between the atrium and peristyle, "what is all this about Valleius Tatinius? I thought you and his wife were intimate friends, and that he was—well, unpleasant perhaps—but eager to please you."

Lydia was grateful for the heavy curtains shielding them from the atrium. She knew that anything she and Ditus said would be private. "Valleius is very angry with me," she confessed. "Angry for the same reason you were angry last night. He thinks I was a fool to invite Paul and the others to stay here. For some reason, he looked on it as a direct insult to him."

Ditus didn't smile. "And so it was. After you had hardly allowed him the privilege of the atrium, you suddenly share your sleeping quarters with strangers."

"Not *my* sleeping quarters," she said sharply, foolishly.

"You know what I mean. They are taken in as family, and the door was closed in his face."

Her voice was bitter. "It's because that's all he ever wanted—access to my sleeping quarters."

Even as she said it, she marveled that she could say this to her son.

But Ditus' reaction was casual. "I told you once that I guessed that. It doesn't surprise me."

"I've carried the burden of it a long time alone," Lydia said slowly. "I wish I had known I could talk to you."

Her honesty seemed to move Ditus to an honesty of his own. "I wouldn't have been very understanding in the beginning—when you needed a confidante most. I've learned a lot this year."

"From Clement." It was a statement, not a question.

"From Clement."

"You mean Clement knows about Valleius?" she asked, suddenly suspicious.

"We've never actually discussed it in so many words." Ditus was being very careful. "But I think he has suspected something."

Lydia remembered Clement's harsh comment on her "fancy Roman friends." Oh, yes, Clement suspected something.

"Tell me, Ditus," Lydia said, glancing at the ugly wound on his forehead, "Tell me, was it because of Valleius you were fighting? Or because of Paul?"

"Paul," he said and stopped abruptly, knowing full well she had trapped him.

"There was gossip?" she asked carefully.

"Not exactly gossip. A couple of soldiers had overheard something—my guess is they heard Valleius talking to his wife—"

"His wife?" Lydia interrupted.

"She had come down to the garrison for something, someone said, and Valleius yelled at her and sent her away. Somebody overheard them, I suppose. They—they threw it up to me."

"And you fought over it?" Her voice was soft. "I wish you could know how sorry I am."

Ditus looked at the floor and his hands twisted together. "I wish *you* could know how *I* felt. I knew you were virtuous —you can't live with someone and not know that—but I believed you to be a fool. It's hard to defend a fool."

"I'm sorry," she said again. If Ditus wasn't giving her respect, he was giving her honesty.

"I still think you're foolish," the boy said bluntly. "But perhaps not a fool. There's a difference."

She found the grace to smile at him. "So tonight, if you had to, you could fight with greater dedication?"

Ditus laughed outright, and it came to her with a distinct shock that she had not heard him laugh often lately.

"I don't know," he confessed ruefully. "I didn't know it hurt so much."

"You were nearly killed, Ditus. You refuse to accept our word about it, about the fact that God healed you. When you see Clement next, ask him. Ask him if your back hadn't been kicked and battered."

Ditus turned his head sharply. "I don't want to talk about that," he said. "I'll admit that Paul isn't quite what I expected he'd be. And I'll even admit that he's magnetic enough to persuade stronger people than you. But that he—or his God—could heal me, that's silly. Things like that don't happen."

"Ask Clement," Lydia said again. "If he carried you home, he'll know."

Ditus was silent a moment and then he said carefully, "I've learned one thing, though. You were probably right about the dangers of gambling and being out at night. Those men would never have dared attack me during the day."

With an effort she kept herself from looking triumphant. "Then I can count on your not going back?"

"I'll probably go a few more times. After another week or so, Clement will start working days part of the time. You understand I went primarily to be with him."

"I understand." Oh, thank you, God, her heart was singing. Thank you for bringing this boy back to me.

"May I ask you something?" Ditus asked. When she nodded, he said, "I have no right to ask it—it's a very intimate question —but it's something I don't understand. How did you —well, avoid getting involved with Valleius? Was it that you didn't like him? Clement says that without love —well, was that it?"

"Not entirely," Lydia admitted. "Valleius is a very exciting and attractive man, and there were times during these past months when I was very lonely. But I have learned about God, and God has given us laws to follow. One of them says, 'Thou shalt not commit adultery.' I couldn't break that law," she finished simply.

"Are you serious?"

"I've never been more so."

"You mean this god you and Minta —this god actually changes your life?"

She smiled. "As much as I'll let him. I'm often hardheaded and determined to go my own way. But if I'll let him, he'll guide me."

Ditus shook his head. "I don't understand you at all."

"But you don't hate me?" She asked the question with sudden fear. She had never dared say anything like that before.

Ditus looked embarrassed. "Of course not. Don't be silly. If I've been —stubborn this year, it's because —because I had to be."

"We've both been stubborn," she said. "Ditus, listen, I've been giving a great deal of thought to the fact that you'll come of age in just a few weeks. You may think I'm not interested, but I am. It's just that I can't figure out how to handle it."

"The traditions are all laid out," he said a little stiffly.

"We need someone to put the toga pura on you," she said.

"I had thought Valleius—" he began.

"No."

"You're right. But surely there's someone."

She nodded. "Of course. We'll find someone. I'll begin to really work on it right away. There's just one thing, Ditus."

"What's that?"

"I can't permit a tribute to be paid to the Roman gods in my home," she said firmly.

"But it's part of the ceremony," he protested. "You don't have to worship them—just place the token in front of a statue."

"No." Her tone was decisive. "The first law of God is 'Thou shalt have no other gods.' I'm sorry, Ditus."

He shrugged. "We'll work it out," he muttered. "Somehow we'll work it out."

"And," she began hesitantly, "I plan to start turning a little of the responsibility of the shop over to you—gradually, of course. But you'll no longer be considered an apprentice."

It wasn't what he wanted, of course. She could tell from the expression on his face. But this was the most she could promise now.

"Thank you," he said, his voice stiff. "I'm grateful for that at least."

"And thank *you*," she cried, "for listening to me. I didn't think you ever gave any thought to me and my problems. You can't know how relieved I am to be able to lean on—on a man again."

"I didn't think you cared what I thought," Ditus said. "You've been so wrapped up in Minta and your religion and the business that I thought—well—" He blundered to a stop.

"You'd better get to bed," she said gently. "I'm sure you're still weak and you must be tired."

"I'm tired," he admitted. "But not really weak at all." He avoided her eyes when he said that. "Tomorrow I'll find a place for Paul to set up his tentmaking before I come to the shop."

It was a mark of the new dignity she'd allowed him to assume, Lydia thought, that enabled him to make the statement without asking if she minded.

"I'm sure Paul will be grateful," was all she said.

Ditus took a small lamp and escorted Lydia to her room. Using his lamp to light the one on her chest, he stood for a brief time looking down at his mother.

"You may be foolish," he said suddenly, sounding very young, "but you're honest and you're brave."

He bent swiftly to kiss her cheek and then turned to hurry to his own room, his lamp making wavering splotches of brightness on the dark walls.

Not until she was nearly asleep did Lydia remember that she had not shared Valleius' threat with Ditus. She had not, as a matter of fact, allowed herself to really think about it. The implications were too terrifying. Somehow, she had to get to Fulvia and beg her not to listen to Valleius' villification of Lydia's character. The question was, how was she going to contact Fulvia?

A casual passerby would have thought she was having a party, Lydia mused a week later, looking around the peristyle. Every bench was filled, and some of the younger people, like David and Minta, were sitting on the ground.

But of course it wasn't a party. The people were here to listen to Paul, to learn about Jesus. At first, Paul had gone out into the city streets to preach. As a following began to grow, Lydia had suggested that they meet at her home during the late afternoon. She was motivated partly by selfishness. Working at the shop, she was unable to listen to what Paul said during the day; but by late afternoon, she, too, could come and join the listeners.

The plan seemed to suit Paul admirably. He spent the early part of each day behind the old houses in the poorer part of the city in a shed which Ditus had found for him. At midafternoon, he came back to Lydia's house to preach to his "congregation," as he called the people who gathered to hear him.

Ditus had grudgingly given his approval to the plan when Lydia asked him, but he refused to join them, refused to listen even when Minta tried to tell him what was being said.

Nor had Lydia been able to contact Fulvia. She had sent messages several times with Pyrus, but he told her that he was turned away at the door without being allowed to deliver the tablet she sent.

Lydia looked around at the people gathered together. In spite of the fact that she wished Ditus and Fulvia were there, in spite of the fact that each knock at her door brought a quick flurry of fear that it might be Valleius, there was still a great sense of satisfaction in her. Paul had promised to continue to tell of the preachings and deeds of Jesus, and the air was almost alive with expectancy. Nowhere else have I found this —this feeling of hope and promise, Lydia thought.

Paul entered the garden-like room and sat on the stool which had been reserved for him.

"Peace in the name of our Lord Jesus," he said.

His face looked tired, Lydia thought, and his shoulders slumped wearily, but his eyes were intent as always.

"Jesus was a master in the art of storytelling," Paul began. "He could take the simplest thing and make of it a great truth. He did it with simple words so that everyone would understand. I can only pray that I can tell it to you as he told it to his followers.

"He told a story once about a sower who went forth to sow." Paul's voice took on a sort of rhythm. "Some of the seed was sown beside the road and the birds ate it. Some fell on rocky soil and grew swiftly but died for lack of good roots. Other seed fell among thorns where they were choked out and produced no crop. But some of the seed fell on good ground and grew to produce a crop thirty, sixty, even a hundred times greater than the original seed."

Paul looked around at the expectant faces. "The disciples of Jesus didn't understand what he meant. You don't seem to, either. Jesus explained that the seed was like the Word of God. Sometimes it falls on the rocky ground of indifference, where Satan deafens the hearers to the truth. Sometimes it falls on hearts that are like the rocky soil. They accept the word with gladness, but when the first difficulty comes, they turn back to their old ways and let the truth die."

Is that the way I've been, Lydia thought humbly. She looked cautiously about her and saw the same concern on a dozen faces. Only Reuben looked totally serene.

Paul went on. "Sometimes the word falls on hearts that are so filled with worry and fear and the concerns of the world that the word of God is choked out and entirely lost."

Once more Lydia felt a twinge of guilt. But no, she comforted herself, she might not be strong every day, but the word of God would never be totally lost in her. Of that she was certain.

"But sometimes," Paul continued, "the word falls on hearts that are rich and fertile and so there grows up a crop of devotion and good deeds and faith."

He paused to ask, "Do you understand?"

"Yes." David was eager. "I've never heard it said so plainly, so clearly."

"Jesus the Christ, through whom all goodness is revealed, is the door through which you can see God," Paul explained.

There was a timid tapping at one of the back doors, and Lydia looked up to catch Kora's eyes. It was odd how normal it seemed to have Kora and Pyrus and the other slaves as part of the group who listened to Paul. How short a time ago it would have seemed presumptuous and wholly irregular.

Kora nodded and slipped from the room. Paul's voice went on, inviting questions, providing answers. As always, he was abrupt, blunt, positive. But under these abrasive qualities, Lydia could sense a thread of tenderness. No wonder the people loved him so, she thought. He is so convicted and convincing that he creates confidence in the weakest of us.

Kora came back into the room, and her eyes sent a message to her mistress. Lydia slipped from her bench and hurried to where Kora was standing.

"What is it?" she whispered.

"It was Mistress Fulvia's slave," Kora said. "She's a cousin of mine, you know, my lady. That would have been her excuse if anyone had seen her coming here."

"What do you mean?" Lydia breathed.

"She had a message from her mistress. Oh, not a written one, my lady. Just a few words. She'll be going to the baths every afternoon, she said."

"Just that? Nothing more?"

"Just that."

"The slave is gone?"

"Yes, my lady."

"Thank you, Kora. Thank you." Lydia's heart was singing as she made her way back to the bench that faced Paul. Fulvia wanted to see her. Fulvia was willing to risk Valleius' anger to see her friend.

I can tell her everything I've learned about Jesus, Lydia thought with a great surge of gratitude. If Fulvia can come to him only through intellect, I now have the words that she needs.

19

Next day, Lydia could hardly wait for the hours to pass until it was time to go to the baths. After lunch, she looked so many times at the sky to observe the movement of the sun that both Ditus and Reuben noticed it and asked what she was expecting to happen. Finally, at least an hour before her regular time to leave the shop, Ditus suggested rather tartly that she ought to leave. He didn't actually say that she was making little or no contribution to the work at hand, but she sensed his implied criticism. She was, however, so anxious to go find Fulvia that she made no retort at all. She merely smiled, waved, and left.

It was her custom to enter the bathhouse by the main front door which could be used by either men or women. But today, like many days recently, she slipped around to the rear entrance used only by women. She decided that it would be wisest to follow the daily routine she had been using since she started to work. She no longer had time for long, relaxing steam baths or the gentle massage that could be obtained from a skilled masseuse. Kora, who had come along today, put Lydia's clothes in the small niche reserved for her while Lydia draped a soft towel around herself and went into the room containing the large pool of hot water. Gratefully, for she was more tired and tense than she realized, she lowered herself into the comforting water.

She did not see Fulvia anywhere, although she scanned every face in as inconspicuous a manner as possible. Just as she stepped out of the water, a slave who looked vaguely familiar came up to her.

"Would you care to come into the women's lounge, my lady?" she asked.

"Yes, in a minute," Lydia returned. "As soon as I'm dressed."

"In the corner by the impluvium," the slave murmured as she hurried away.

Lydia's hands were shaking as she helped Kora in the adjusting and draping of her stola. Yesterday, in her deep joy at receiving a message from Fulvia, she had not even considered it might be bad news. Now it suddenly occurred to her that Fulvia might be bringing a warning about Valleius.

"Don't worry, my lady," Kora begged. "Things will work out all right. Our God will protect you."

Why was it necessary, Lydia thought, that she was always in need of reassurance from children and slaves? Did her own inadequacies sit so obviously on her?

The lounge was full of chattering, laughing women, and for a minute Lydia failed to see Fulvia. Then a gesture caught her eyes. Beyond the impluvium, which was cool and shadowed, filled with rainwater, Fulvia was waiting on a secluded bench.

Oh, God, please! Lydia begged, aware that her small prayer included a dozen requests. Then she spoke to Fulvia. "Greetings," she said breathlessly.

"Lydia, my dear," Fulvia said, and her voice was as warm as it had ever been.

With a little sob of relief, Lydia reached out to take Fulvia's hands. But it would never do to let others even guess that this might be an emotional meeting. "You're well?" she asked.

"I've missed seeing you," Fulvia said in a clear, carrying voice, "but I know how hard you've been working. You must plan a whole day off sometime soon so that we can visit the library together."

It was certainly an ordinary enough greeting, and if anyone had stopped chattering long enough to listen to them, Fulvia's words would have disarmed them.

"Indeed I hope to soon," Lydia said, entering into the game. "Now, tell me, what do you hear from young Arturus in Rome?"

In less than a minute, the conversations of all the other women had built a wall around Lydia and Fulvia so that they were able to lower their voices and say the things they wanted to say.

"Valleius is very angry," Fulvia said. "He has Nuba posted outside the main gate of the baths most days to see whether or not you're meeting me."

"I've been coming in the back door," Lydia said. "I just felt I should. I suppose it was God telling me what to do."

"Something very strange has happened," Fulvia said in a soft, quick voice. "Nuba has become enamored of your friend Paul. He and Erosa have taken to following them around. He pretends it's because Erosa wants to do it, but I overheard him talking to the other slaves. He *believes* in this Jewish Messiah. Nuba! I can't quite accept it all."

"I know," Lydia said. "Some of my slaves have even been baptized. But you knew that, I guess. When Paul preaches in the evening, the slaves join the listeners. Paul says that in the eyes of God, all people are equal."

"And Paul has continued to tell you about the man, Jesus?"

It was the question Lydia had been waiting for. All the rest had simply been a prelude to the opportunity for which she had been praying.

"Oh, Fulvia, listen," she began. "I've gathered up every

word, praying constantly that I would have a chance to tell you. Paul told us once that Jesus said that we ought to love God with all our heart and all our soul and all our *mind*. It's all right for you to need to *know*."

"Truly?" Fulvia's face expressed hope.

"Yes, truly." The two women were so oblivious to the passing of time that when Kora came up to touch Lydia's shoulder, they were startled to realize that the light shining down from the opening in the roof had shifted. It must be late afternoon.

"My lady," Kora said apologetically. "You have talked for a very long time. The people will be waiting for you and worried."

Fulvia had a dazed look on her face. "We have to talk more," she said. "I have to hear everything."

"Tomorrow?" Lydia suggested.

"Yes. Earlier tomorrow. Can you come earlier?"

"As early as you wish," Lydia said recklessly.

"Would I dare come to the shop just before noon?" Fulvia asked. "I could make sure that Valleius was nowhere around, and we could go back into the storeroom where no one could see us."

"Perfect," Lydia agreed. "If you think it's safe, that is."

"I have a feeling," Fulvia said slowly, "that Jesus is someone a person has to be willing to take risks for."

Speechlessly, Lydia reached to grip Fulvia's hands. Her eyes were brimming with tears.

"Till tomorrow," Fulvia said and hurried toward the front of the building.

"Go to the back door," Lydia directed Kora. "When you're sure that there are no Tatinius slaves in the vicinity, call me and we'll go out that way."

The people were already gathered at Lydia's house when she arrived. She slipped in unobtrusively and sat on one of the back benches. She didn't even allow herself to think about the fact that Valleius' attitude had not changed and that an open friendship with Fulvia might be difficult or even impossible. She merely hugged to herself the wonderful knowledge that Fulvia wanted to find her way to the knowledge of Jesus Christ. Some of us come by way of our hearts, Lydia reflected, remembering her own impulsive push toward the river, and some of us more cautiously by way of our minds. The important thing is that we come. She had settled back to listen to Paul when the movement of another latecomer caught her eye. She glanced casually toward the man who had come in and then felt a shock like lightning go through her body. It was Ditus!

The boy—how automatically she had assumed the newcomer was a man, she thought, before she recognized him—sat as far away from Paul as it was possible to sit and still be in the same room. His eyes darted apprehensively from side to side, and he refused even to glance in his mother's direction.

But he's here, Lydia exulted. He's here! Oh, God, put the words that Ditus needs into Paul's mouth. She glanced at Reuben, saw that he had recognized Ditus and that his lips were moving. So were Minta's. With so many praying, Lydia thought, closer to laughter than anything else, you don't have a chance, my son. You'll end up being God's child, after all.

But when Paul's sermon was ended and several people came forward for baptism, Ditus was not among them. Lydia swung her head around and saw that Ditus' place was empty. Her own keen disappointment was mirrored on the faces of Reuben and Minta, who were obviously also looking for Ditus.

"The boy's like a wild pony," Luke said, suddenly at her elbow. "He won't come quietly or easily as his sister did. He'll buck and shy and run away and kick up his heels. But if he ever accepts the bit, he'll be the most biddable of all."

The analogy was strangely apt, Lydia realized. She was

just expecting too much, thinking that Ditus would come running at the first exposure to Paul. Ditus, like Fulvia, could come only in his own way, in his own time.

She tried to say this to Luke, and he smiled. "Or in God's own time," he suggested.

"Yes, of course," Lydia nodded. "It's wrong of me to expect instant miracles."

"Not wrong," Paul said. He had come up to them and had evidently overheard. "God causes instant miracles to happen, too. One of your problems, my friend, is that you try to foresee every conceivable solution to every problem. You haven't learned to turn things over to God."

"I try to," Lydia said, feeling chastened.

"Then you must try harder," Paul said. "You must strive daily until your love for God is perfect."

He turned away then to speak to someone else. Luke's eyes were compassionate.

"Paul hasn't time for a slow, gentle approach," Luke explained. "Don't be hurt by him. He feels that he must go straight to the heart of every problem. Sometimes he's painfully blunt."

"But honest," Lydia said. "And in this instance, right. I know how often I fail."

"How often we all fail," Luke said, his voice warm and comforting.

When Fulvia came into the shop the next day, she said she was sure she had not been followed. Valleius was at the garrison and had indicated he'd be there all day. Nuba and Erosa had gone out against Valleius' orders, but when the girl was lucid, or as lucid as she ever was, Fulvia declared, she wept to see Paul again; and when she was mad, she got hysterical if Nuba didn't do as she demanded.

"I hope they get home safely before Valleius does," Fulvia said. She moved her shoulders in a little shrug. "I think Erosa is really becoming harder for Valleius to handle, which only makes him more possessive and protective of her. She still brings in a large income, and he believes that the madder she gets, the more surely she will prophesy."

"I just hope she doesn't cause any more trouble," Lydia said.

"I, too. But, now, tell me more of the things you promised to tell."

The two-hour noontime period sped by with the same swiftness they had known at the baths. By the time it ended, Lydia was sure Fulvia had been won over to her own belief that Jesus was indeed the son of God and that he had been raised from the dead. If a meeting could be arranged with Paul or Silas, Lydia was confident Fulvia would be baptized.

But Fulvia was not ready for such a meeting yet. "Give me a little time," she begged, as they heard the shutters being opened in the shops along the colonnaded walk. "Until Valleius has something else on his mind. Right now, he's constantly spying on me."

"All right," Lydia said. "But don't wait too long."

A sudden shrill outcry from the street, followed by a babble of voices and the sound of a crowd gathering, made Lydia's heart lurch with dread. With a slight motion that told Fulvia to stay where she was, Lydia hurried out to the stoa. What she saw made her catch her breath in fear. Paul and Silas were walking across the square, evidently returning from their lunch. Beside them were Nuba and Erosa. The girl must have cried out at first sight of Paul, and now she was running eagerly beside him, her voice raised in a shrill proclamation.

Paul looked tired and irritated, not in any mood to tolerate the nuisance of the girl's insanity. Although Silas was murmuring soothingly in his ear, Paul's shoulders twitched impatiently, as though he wanted to shake off the annoyance.

But what turned Lydia's blood to ice was the sight of

Valleius hurrying across the square from the opposite direction. As Lydia watched, she saw Valleius catch sight of his slaves. His step quickened, and Lydia turned to race breathlessly back into the storeroom.

"Here," she panted to Fulvia, "hurry! Go out this back door, run along the little alley behind the shops until you come to the far side of the square. If you go through the narrow arched doorway on your left, you'll come out right behind the bathhouse. You can slip in the women's door and no one will know you've been here."

"Why the alley?" Fulvia began with distaste on her face.

But Lydia was almost frantic. "Don't ask questions. Go! Paul's out there. With Erosa and Nuba. And Valleius is coming toward them from the garrison!"

Fulvia gasped and the color left her face. "Oh, God help us," she cried in soft anguish and fled out the back door of the shop.

Lydia prayed as she hurried toward the stoa. "Almighty God," she whispered, "please don't let anything happen. Don't let anything happen to Paul. Please!"

Her words had barely been formed when she heard Erosa's voice, shrill and strident. "These men are the servants of the Most High God, which show us the way of salvation!"

Lydia moved fearfully to the arched opening of the stoa, just in time to see Paul turn with exasperation toward Erosa.

"I command thee in the name of Jesus Christ to come out of her!" he shouted in a strong, authoritative voice.

Erosa stopped in her tracks. A look of utter terror spread across her face. She grasped her throat with her two hands as though she were strangling.

Nuba turned pleadingly to Paul. "Don't be angry with her, sir. She's mad and can't help herself."

Paul looked exhausted. "I'm not angry with *her*. I'm

angry with the demons which possess her. They're evil. Come out, I say."

Erosa's eyes widened and a shrill wail issued from her mouth. Suddenly she crumpled into a heap on the ground.

Nuba knelt beside the girl, but Paul's voice stopped him before he could pick her up.

"Don't touch her yet. It will take a minute or two until the demons are all out of her. Then you can take her home. In a short time, she'll be as normal as any girl."

"What do you mean, 'as normal as any girl'?" The sudden harsh sound of Valleius' voice sent terror plunging through Lydia.

Paul looked disdainfully at the angry Roman. "I mean, she will never again be tormented by the demons which have plagued her."

"You can't be serious?" Valleius' face was an ugly brick red.

Paul shrugged. "Wait and see," he said.

At that moment, Erosa sat up. Her small face was tranquil and peaceful, her eyes lucid and shining. She looked up at Paul.

"Master," she said.

"I'm your master and don't you forget it," Valleius shouted.

Erosa looked at him with a sweet but puzzled expression. "Oh, no, sir," she said firmly. "I never saw you before in all my life."

Before Lydia could close her eyes against the horror, she saw Valleius' foot launched in a furious kick at Erosa's head. She'll be killed, Lydia thought, and through a mist of terror she saw the dark form of Nuba's body as he threw himself protectingly over the girl.

20

Lydia was never sure whether the scream she heard came from her own throat or from Erosa or from one of the women who had gathered in the square. Valleius' foot thudded against Nuba's body and the slave groaned in pain. Furious, Valleius grabbed Nuba's hair to jerk him off the cringing Erosa.

"How dare you?" Valleius panted. "I'll have you whipped until you'll be screaming for mercy."

He flung Nuba to one side, and Lydia was shocked at the incredible strength of the Roman.

"Now, let me at her," Valleius cried, reaching for Erosa.

Incredibly, Nuba threw himself again on top of the girl. Even more incredibly, Silas and Paul grabbed Valleius' arms and held him back.

"Don't punish the girl," Paul commanded in so forceful a tone that Valleius was momentarily halted. "If you must punish anyone, punish me."

"You think I won't?" Valleius shouted. "All of you —you and that devil, Nuba, who dares to defy me, and the girl — you'll all feel the whip before this is over."

More and more people were crowding around, attracted by the shouting. Lydia realized that for a moment Erosa and Nuba were separated from Valleius by a surging wall of curious people.

"Nuba," she called, her voice barely above a whisper.

She couldn't really believe he'd hear her over the general commotion, but he did. She beckoned and he seemed to understand at once. With a swift motion, he pulled Erosa to her feet. Shielding her with his body, he whispered urgently in her ear. She stood without moving while Nuba darted in the opposite direction from Lydia, shouting as he went, "Run, Erosa. Toward the bath. Down past the library. Run."

Every head in the crowd, including Valleius', Paul's, and Silas', swung to look in the direction Nuba had suggested. In the instant that all backs were turned, Erosa fled, silent as a shadow, toward Lydia. Without hesitation, Lydia grabbed her and pulled her toward the storeroom. Quickly, breathlessly, she pushed the girl under the cutting table, behind a pile of bolts that were stacked on the floor.

"Stay there!" she hissed. "Don't move."

Erosa's voice was soft and as sane as Minta's. "Yes, my lady. Don't worry."

Lydia walked with an attempt at casualness toward the front of the stoa again. But her heart was hammering with heavy, thick strokes.

"What's all the confusion?" she called in a clear, light voice. "Is something wrong?"

Valleius turned sharply in her direction. "Have you seen Erosa?"

"Erosa? Isn't she over there with Nuba?"

Valleius pulled himself away from the restraining hands of Paul and Silas. "You can see she isn't. How long have you been standing there?"

"Just a second. I heard a great deal of shouting and came out to see what was the matter."

"I'll find her," Valleius said grimly. "She can't have gone far." He turned to Paul and Silas and to Nuba, who was on all fours on the ground where Valleius must have knocked him. "And when I do...." His voice trailed off. Looking around he caught sight of several policemen in the crowd. "Here!" he called. "You—and you. Take these men. Hold them as my prisoners while I get another magistrate to help me pass judgment. No leniency," he instructed as the policemen came up to him. "Tie these three and make them kneel here in the square until I come back."

Lydia's heart constricted with pity. Paul should not be forced to endure this kind of punishment. So intent was she on the horror of what was going on in the square that she hardly noticed Ditus when he brushed by her and went into the storeroom. Too late she realized she should have kept him in the stoa. She turned to call him, but Valleius suddenly strode over to her. "Have you hidden the girl?" he asked roughly.

"I?" Lydia stared at him with an expression that she could only hope was one of astonishment and not fear. "Why should I do that? You know how I've felt about her. She's been a source of nothing but trouble to me. Why would I shelter her?"

"To hurt me," Valleius snapped.

"I don't want to hurt you," Lydia protested.

"No? By Jupiter, you certainly have funny ways of showing your concern for me."

"Valleius," she began, putting out her hand to touch his arm.

He shook her off with an angry gesture. "I've been a fool," he said shortly. "I've been sentimental and stupid about you. Thinking maybe you might change. Where is she?"

The abrupt question and the brutal twist he gave her wrist made Lydia gasp with mingled surprise and pain. "How would I know?" she cried.

"Take me into the storeroom," Valleius barked. He didn't even glance over his shoulder to where the policemen had forced their three prisoners onto their knees on the rough cobbles.

"Take me," Valleius insisted, his fingers digging into her wrist.

Cringing from the pain, Lydia led the way into the storeroom. If Ditus hadn't discovered Erosa, perhaps Valleius wouldn't find her either.

The storeroom was empty! Lydia looked around dazedly. Surely she had not just imagined Ditus moving silently through the stoa. But where was he?

"Is she under here?" Valleius asked sharply. To her alarm, he moved purposefully toward the cutting table.

"Under where?" she quavered.

"Don't act stupid." With an abrupt motion, Valleius thrust Lydia from him and jerked the table from the wall.

Oh, God, Lydia thought, oh, please!

There was nothing and no one under the table. Valleius swore and moved rapidly around the room, looking in every corner where the girl might have been hidden.

"I was wrong," Valleius said. "I'm not often wrong. You had guilt all over your face."

"I don't know what you're talking about," Lydia said, her fear making her voice tremble so that it sounded truly bewildered.

Valleius came over to Lydia and grabbed her arms, forcing her to look up at him. "Don't try me any further," he said in a hard, cold voice. "Maybe when you see what I plan to do to your Jewish friends, you'll be sorry you didn't take *me* in instead of them."

Incredibly, he bent his head and kissed her, his mouth cruel and punishing.

Then, abruptly he turned and left her. She heard him stalk across the stoa out into the street. "Keep them kneeling," he called to the policemen, and then he was gone.

Lydia leaned weakly against the table. In all her life she had never known real fear —the kind of fear that paralyzes and renders helpless —until this minute.

Where are you, God, she thought. I prayed so desperately that nothing would happen to Paul, but you didn't listen. What kind of God are you?

A sudden sound at the door of the storeroom made Lydia look up to see Ditus, followed by Reuben, coming in.

"Mother," Ditus said, his voice very calm and normal, "are you all right? Why are Paul and Silas being treated as common criminals in front of the shop? What's happened?"

Lydia looked at him, bewildered. She opened her mouth to ask questions of her own when suddenly something in Ditus' expression alerted her. The boy was putting on an act for someone. Someone in the stoa?

"I don't know," Lydia said calmly and saw the relief and approval on her son's face. "There was a great deal of shouting, and Valleius came storming into the stoa after telling the policemen to hold Paul and Silas. And Nuba, too."

She stopped a minute and then went on. "For some reason, he searched the storeroom. Of course he found nothing. But he was very abusive."

Ditus sighed with evident relief. "I wish you'd go home, Mother. Things may be very unpleasant around here. I'd feel better if you went home."

For the first time, Reuben spoke, and Lydia was shocked to see how white and old he looked. "The boy's right, Lydia. You ought to go home."

"Am I needed at home?" Lydia asked steadily.

She knew that Ditus would understand. If she had grasped the idea, without any words or signs, that he had helped Erosa escape, then Ditus would surely understand that she was asking whether the girl was in their house.

"Perhaps not *needed*," Ditus conceded. "Miriam has everything under control." The last five words were said so low and rapidly that they could not be heard beyond the storeroom.

"Then I'll stay here," Lydia declared, her voice firm. "Do

you think I could let Paul and Silas be mistreated at my door and just run away?"

"It won't be a pretty sight," Ditus warned.

"They'll need to know I'm here, that I care."

Reuben shook his head and she went over to him solicitously. "You look exhausted, my dear, dear friend. It's you who ought to go home."

"I can be as stubborn as you," Reuben answered. His voice was breathless and shaky. "They'll need my prayers."

"Some strong Roman authority would achieve a lot more than prayers," Ditus said rudely, but he could not keep the distress from showing in his face.

"Will they be beaten?" Lydia asked in a low voice.

"They'll be beaten," Ditus said. "That's what happens when one defies the authority of Rome."

Reuben stepped to the door. "There's no one in the stoa," he said softly.

But Ditus' eyes indicated the door that opened onto the alley. "I'm going out front, Mother. I'd be grateful if you would stay back here."

"I'll try," was all Lydia could promise.

The noise of the crowd increased minute by minute. Reuben, white and sick looking, stayed with Lydia for a short time and then he went out through the stoa as Ditus had done. Lydia waited beside the cutting table, listening to the ugly mob sounds outside. There was no one, it seemed, who would speak in favor of these wandering Jews, no one who would offer to defend them when the impromptu trial started. Knowing how the Roman magistrates functioned —one hand washing the other—Lydia was certain that when Valleius came back with his fellow magistrates, the decision would be unanimous.

In the meantime, Paul and Silas were kneeling on the

stones. I can't bear it, Lydia thought. Filling a small pitcher with water, she hurried to the front of the stoa to offer the prisoners a cool drink.

She was too late. Just as she reached the point where she could see what was going on, she saw Valleius and several other men striding rapidly from the garrison toward the square. Behind them came two policemen carrying the thin, flexible, tough wooden rods which were used to whip prisoners. A cold, thick nausea churned suddenly in Lydia's stomach, and she ran, ashamed at her weakness, to the back door, thoroughly sick.

I can't bear it, she kept saying to herself, feeling her teeth chatter. There was a sudden silence, and then Valleius' voice carried clearly, even to the rear of the storeroom.

"These men, being Jews, are throwing our city into confusion. They are proclaiming customs which it's not lawful for us, as Romans, to accept. I demand a punishment for them."

If he had only been honest, Lydia thought achingly, if he had said that he was punishing these men because they had taken away the income he derived from Erosa's prophesying, it might have been more bearable. But to blame Paul and Silas for something they had not even done was reprehensible. Oddly enough, her disgust at Valleius seemed to give her strength. She straightened and wiped her mouth, and with her head up, she hurried to the stoa again.

"They have only preached about God," Reuben cried. His voice was thin and feeble against the growing angry roar of the crowd. Someone shoved him and he stumbled and nearly fell. His thin, old hands pressed convulsively against his chest, but he persisted in pushing to the front of the mob. "They are only priests." Reuben's voice was shrill and shaking.

"Shut up!" one of the policemen shouted and elbowed the old man out of the way. "How many stripes?" The question was put eagerly to Valleius.

"How many?" Valleius asked, turning with seeming concern to his fellow magistrates. "Thirty? Forty?"

They might have said only ten, Lydia thought, but Valleius had put his poison into their minds.

"Forty," the men agreed.

The thin rods began their silent ascent and whistling descent. For only a minute Lydia stood frozen, watching the thin bloody welts appear one by one on Nuba's black back, on Silas' back, on Paul's bent shoulders.

Why don't they scream, Lydia thought. She saw Paul's head jerk up at the first blow and saw his lips form words, but the roar of the crowd prevented her from hearing.

"Oh, God," Lydia cried out in agony. "Oh, please."

She looked up to see Ditus coming toward her, his hands stretched out, a look of pity on his face. But just before he reached her, she felt a dark wave of oblivion sweeping over her. Weakly, cravenly, she welcomed its black embrace and let herself crumple to the floor in a faint.

21

Lydia had only a vague, blurred memory of being taken from the shop to her home. Her mind simply refused to accept the dreadful scene that had taken place in the square, and a merciful oblivion kept her from seeing Paul, Silas, and Nuba beaten and bloody, staggering between the policemen on their way to prison.

For several hours, she lay passively on her bed and wept silently. Minta, whose face was white from the enormity of what Ditus had told her when he brought Lydia home, sat beside her mother and and placed cool, wet clothes across her eyes and talked in a soft, soothing little voice.

"Paul will be all right," Minta said. "Truly, Mother. Men are whipped every week in the square and they live. I know it seems so terrible because it's Paul and Silas, but they'll be made strong by God. I know they will."

"I prayed," Lydia said in a clogged voice. "I asked God not to let anything happen to Paul. But it happened anyhow."

"There might have been a reason," Minta suggested, stroking Lydia's hand.

"What reason could there be for beating a man who did nothing wrong?"

"Mother, I don't know. How could I know? But you can't really say Paul did nothing. He took away Valleius' source of income—as surely as though he had wrecked a store."

Lydia opened her swollen eyes. "Are you condoning what Valleius has done?"

"No, oh, no, Mother. I'm only trying to explain how it could seem to him."

Lydia was silent a minute, feeling the helpless tears slipping down her face. Suddenly she asked the question that had been in the back of her mind ever since Valleius dragged her into the storeroom. "What happened to Erosa?"

Minta looked over her shoulder and leaned closer to the bed. "Ditus helped her run away. He took her straight to Miriam's."

"But she won't be safe there. Valleius will surely find her."

Minta's eyes shone. "Miriam has some hair that was cut from her head when she was a girl and her family escaped from persecution. It's long and straight and they've made a sort of wig out of it. When Erosa puts it on with a square of cloth bound around her forehead, and a little darkener on her skin, she looks nothing at all like Valleius' slave. The expression on her face, Ditus says, is like that of another girl altogether."

"How did Ditus know she was under the table?"

"He saw her run toward the shop, he says, and guessed that's where you'd hide her. He just flew in and grabbed her and raced down the alley. Of course, I know that God was helping him, but he doesn't know that yet."

Lydia's voice was tired and a little bitter. "Doesn't it seem strange to you that God would help a nonbeliever and let his most faithful servant be publicly whipped?"

Minta's face was serene. "No, not really. I can't begin to understand. But I *know* God cares."

Lydia felt the touch of shame. "I envy you your constant faith," she whispered.

"But, Mother, it was you who brought me to God."

Lydia closed her eyes again. Another thought flashed into her mind. "Why did Ditus do what he did? Why did he help Erosa instead of Valleius?" she said.

"I think probably Ditus is—well, terribly attracted to Erosa. He has always thought she was the most beautiful girl he's ever seen. I've heard she's of high birth but was sold into slavery because she is—or was—mad. One of Ditus' biggest quarrels with the idea of God was Erosa's madness. But now that she's sane and more beautiful than ever, well—" Minta just grinned and spread her hands in a resigned gesture.

Lydia's tired mind reeled under this new shock. Was there no end to the unexpected events in her life?

It was just at that moment that Luke came to her door.

Lydia struggled to sit up. "You've heard about Paul and Silas?" she cried.

"Yes. I can't do anything about that now. I'm hoping that later—but I have something even worse to tell you now."

She stared at him, stricken. "How could anything be worse?" she protested.

Luke sat down on the edge of the bed and took Lydia's hand in his. He reached over with his other hand and took Minta's. "It's Reuben," he said very gravely, very gently.

"Oh, please," Lydia cried, "he's not dead? Please don't tell me he's dead." She was seeing in memory the sick, white, old face, the thin hands clutching his chest.

"Not dead," Luke said, "but dying. He's calling for you. Will you come?"

"Oh, yes." Somehow she found the strength to struggle up from her bed.

"Wait, wait a minute," Luke said. "Shall we pray for strength, we three?"

Lydia and Minta nodded, and, linked by clasped hands, they prayed for the courage they would need. Then Lydia went hastily to the basin to splash cold water in her eyes so that she would look better for Reuben.

"Let's hurry," she begged, and Minta and Luke came to walk beside her down the steps and out into the late afternoon. Pyrus and Kora were waiting at the door; it seemed natural that both of them should come along. Pyrus would be needed if they had to come home after dark, Lydia reflected, and Kora, too, might be able to help in the hours that lay ahead.

Miriam, Silas, and David were the only people in Reuben's small house. Almost indifferently, Lydia saw David reach out his arms to comfort Minta, who went trustingly into his embrace. Perhaps she didn't have to worry about that anymore. Perhaps Minta's feeling for the boy had gone too far ever to be called back. Well, she'd work it all out later.

Now, all her concern was centered on the old man who lay like a dried strip of parchment on his narrow bed. His breathing was ragged and shallow, and his face was the color of tallow.

"Reuben!" Lydia went to her knees beside the bed and put her arms around him. "Reuben, I'm here."

His eyes fluttered open, and to her amazement a wide smile lit his face. "Lydia. My dear daughter. You've come."

"Of course I've come."

"I thought you might be trying to help Paul," Reuben murmured.

The words sliced at Lydia with a new pain. It's what she should have been doing. Instead, she had been lying on her bed, weeping, wallowing in the luxury of self-pity.

She couldn't tell that to Reuben. "I'm not sure yet what to do," she said humbly. "But when I'm sure you're all right, then I'll start trying to get Paul out of prison."

"I'm dying," Reuben said in a weak but clear tone.

"Nonsense. I won't let you die." She tried to make her words confident and cheerful.

"Lydia, my dear, I don't have time for dishonesty. I want to—leave you with truth and dignity."

"I don't want to upset you by crying," she gasped, trying desperately to hold back her tears.

"There's nothing wrong with tears...you loved me... you'll miss me. Crying—is—normal." In spite of his breath-lessness, his eyes were clear and aware.

"Oh, Reuben." She put her head on his thin chest and heard the frightening plunge and stumble of his heart.

His hand brushed over her hair. "You've been a good daughter in my old age. I've been afraid...I'd die alone... no one to care." His voice slurred and slowed. He closed his eyes for a minute and then looked around the room. "But I'm not alone. God's people, *my* people." His mouth curved again in a grateful smile.

"Isn't there anything you can do?" Lydia begged Luke.

"There's nothing anyone can do." Reuben's voice was suddenly strong again. "Don't grieve long, my child. You surely know we will see each other again."

She had heard of the promise from Paul, and it had been a thing she could believe in an academic way. These words were different. Reuben stood in the shadow of death, his hands already getting cold, but there was such an affirma-tion in his words that Lydia felt an altogether different kind of hope.

"Truly, Reuben? Do you truly believe that?"

"Didn't Jesus say so? To the thief on the cross?" His voice was so weak that she had to lean close to hear him. It took a long time for the words to come out. "If I didn't believe, could I leave you without grief?"

"Then I'll be able to stand it —knowing I'll see you again," she declared.

"And you'll never stop believing?"

"Never," she promised.

"Sometimes you do," Reuben said, his ragged voice gently accusing.

"I know," she confessed. "I know."

"I have no money to leave you, no inheritance, but I leave you my faith. Take it and wear it—like a shield against danger."

"I will," she whispered. "Oh, Reuben, I will."

There was a film growing in his eyes. The light is going out, Lydia thought in panic.

"I love you," she cried, lest he leave her with the words unsaid.

He smiled and his lips formed the words, "I love you, too," but there was no sound.

"I can't bear it," Lydia said abruptly. "I just can't bear it."

"God will meet your every need," Reuben whispered, reprovingly. "Jesus will give you—" The voice stopped abruptly, chopped off by a long, whistling breath.

And the light went out.

Lydia stared into the blank eyes where the essence of Reuben was no longer discernible. "He's gone," she whispered.

Luke's hands gently closed the empty eyes. "He lives," he said quietly.

Lydia felt an unexpected warmth growing in her. She had expected to feel cold and drained and hollow as she had felt when Aurelius died. Instead, there was this warmth filling her with an incredible lightness and sense of well-being.

The tears continued to fall down her face, but she knew she was smiling with joy.

"I won't really have to get along without him," she announced in a tone of discovery. "He'll never really leave me."

Luke crossed Reuben's hands on his chest and pulled a thin cover up over his face. "If ever a man died in the certainty of God..." he murmured.

Lydia looked around. Minta was holding David's hand and mopping at her tears. Miriam stood quietly at the foot of the bed, letting her tears flow unchecked.

Lydia felt a sudden stab of guilt. "He didn't say good-bye to anyone but me," she said humbly. "I took all his attention."

"No," Miriam said gently. "You're wrong. He had already said his farewells to all of us. He was waiting for you. He couldn't let go until you came."

"He told a story once," Lydia said, "about Elijah and Elisha, and how Elijah put his mantle on Elisha. I feel as though Reuben has put his mantle on me."

There was a slight motion in the far corner of the room, and Lydia caught a glimpse of a girl with long, straight hair and a sober, gentle look on her face.

Probably a friend of Miriam's, Lydia thought, and turned her attention away. It was Minta who went up to the girl and took her hands. "I'm glad you're safe," she said, her voice catching on a sob.

"Thank you."

The voice did not sound familiar, but the meaning of Minta's words suddenly hit Lydia.

"Is this —Erosa?" Lydia whispered, staring.

"Shh!" Miriam's voice was low. "This is my niece, Rebekkah, recently arrived from Jerusalem. She speaks little or no Greek." Miriam's eyes were filled with warning.

And Lydia understood. Rising from her knees, she hesitated a moment before she pulled back the cover to kiss Reuben's forehead. Then she turned to the girl.

"Welcome, Rebekkah," she said. "You may not understand me, but I'm glad you're here."

The girl's eyes filled with tears and she quickly bent her head and kissed Lydia's hands. "If it were not for you," she whispered brokenly.

If it were not for you.

Lydia stood in utter stillness while her thoughts raced. She had been the one around whom and through whom all of these events had happened. God must have a task for her to do, and until this moment she had done it only fumblingly and by accident.

It would be different now. Shored up and strengthened by Reuben's last gift of faith, she would do God's will in a new and purposeful way. And she would begin with Paul.

"Pray for me," she announced. "I'm going to the home of Valleius Tatinius to see if I can get Paul released. Pyrus, you come with me. Luke, will you and David see that Minta and Miriam and —and Rebekkah are taken safely home?"

She turned with purpose and resolution and walked out into the dark and empty streets of Philippi.

22

"You're wasting your time." Valleius' voice was cold. He stared at Lydia with mingled disdain and anger.

"I'm sorry about Erosa," Lydia said. "I know she was worth a lot of money to you. Perhaps I could manage to repay some of your loss if you'd release Paul."

"I'd hardly accept a bribe from you," Valleius said with contempt. "Even if I needed the money. Which I don't. The income from Erosa was —an extra luxury. That's all."

"Then why have you been so harsh with Paul and Silas if the loss of the money doesn't matter to you?"

"Because I choose to and because it's in my power to do it," Valleius said flatly.

"Do you realize that you killed Reuben in the process?" Lydia cried, fully realizing the truth of what she was saying for the first time. "It was the shock of seeing Paul beaten which killed him."

"Good," Valleius said indifferently and watched with satisfaction as the horror filled Lydia's eyes.

"I didn't know you were like this," she whispered in disbelief.

"You know very little about me. You never gave me the chance to teach you."

"You've been teaching *me* for twenty-five years," Fulvia said coldly, appearing suddenly at the doorway. "And even I don't know you."

"Go to your room, my dear." Valleius' voice was even.

"This is something strictly between Lydia and me."

Fulvia advanced into the room. "No, it's among all of us. If I'm not an admitted follower of Paul, it isn't because I don't believe."

Valleius stared at his wife. "You wouldn't dare go against my wishes," he announced.

"Oh, but I would," Fulvia said. "If you find this impossible to live with, then a divorce is the only way out."

Valleius drew in his breath with a sharp, hissing sound. Lydia found herself remembering gossip she had heard long ago which said that Fulvia's dowry had been enormous and had been left in trust to her by an eccentric father. Valleius had brought social standing into the marriage but not money. With Erosa gone, he couldn't possibly afford to give up Fulvia.

"Don't talk foolishness," Valleius said sharply. "What about the boys? What about all—the good things we've shared? How can you even talk of leaving me?"

"I didn't say anything about leaving you. I merely said that if you couldn't allow me the freedom I need to worship God, we would have to separate. I imagine you would be the one to do the leaving."

"This is something we can discuss when we're alone," Valleius snapped.

"Why?" Fulvia's voice was cool and sweetly reasonable. "If you have considered Lydia worthy of your attention for a year, why shut her out now?"

Lydia's heart jerked as Valleius swung toward her. "What have you told her?"

Lydia opened her mouth to speak but Fulvia cut in quickly. "She hasn't told me anything. But do you think I'm a fool? Wives have a way of detecting that sort of thing." Lydia made a move to protest, but Fulvia silenced her with a smile. "Oh, I know nothing happened. I have eyes to see."

"I won't be exposed to this drivel!" Valleius shouted, veins bulging in his neck from the anger that choked him. "Neither one of you is even intelligent. One can put up with a fool in a wife, but to have to face it in —"

"A *friend*?" Fulvia suggested caustically.

"Be quiet!" Valleius thundered. "I'll talk to you later. As for *you*," he swung back to Lydia. "The answer to your request is no and no and *no*! I will release Paul when and if I feel like it. At this moment, I can only say I hope he rots in the stocks."

"Stocks?" Lydia had heard of the agony of the stocks that sometimes forced prisoners' legs so far apart that their hips were dislocated.

"I told your friend, Clement, to put them all in wooden stocks. If you think kneeling on the cobbles was bad, you must be taken to see the stocks. As a matter of fact, I'll see to it tomorrow. I'll see to a lot of things," he promised, his voice thick with rage. "Now, get out of here."

Lydia turned to go. Fulvia ran across the room to her. "I'm sorry," she said breathlessly. "Something can be worked out. I know it can. What were you saying about Reuben just as I came into the room?"

"He's dead," Lydia announced dully.

"Oh, no!" Fulvia grabbed at Lydia while quick tears wet her cheeks. "Not Reuben."

"It was the shock of seeing Paul beaten," Lydia said steadily. "Perhaps your husband can explain it all away."

"I don't need to explain anything," Valleius shouted. "Are you getting out of here?"

"Yes, I'm going. Goodnight, my dear," Lydia said to Fulvia.

Fulvia held herself very straight as though she would crumple if she moved. "Goodnight, Lydia," she said through stiff lips. "I'll try to see you tomorrow or the next day."

"Fulvia!" Valleius threatened.

"As I said, Valleius. There is always divorce."

Lydia looked at the man and woman facing her and then turned and fled. Pyrus was waiting by the door so he had probably heard everything. At one time, she thought dazedly, that idea wouldn't even have occured to her.

"Will he hurt her, do you think?" Lydia asked.

"No, my lady. He's a shrewd and cunning man. He would be far more apt to woo her than to hurt her."

Lydia stared in astonishment at Pyrus' face, dim in the wavering light of the lamp. "How do you know so much?" she asked.

"Slaves listen," he explained. "We know more than our masters. We've just never admitted it."

"I'm frightened," Lydia confessed. "I've never been so frightened before. I don't know what to do."

"Perhaps you should just go home," Pyrus suggested.

Lydia thought for a minute. "All right. We'll go home long enough to get wine and cheese and fruit. And ointment. Luke will have it. He and Timothy can come with us. We'll go to the jail."

"At night, my lady? A woman out on the streets at night?"

"With you and Luke and Timothy, I'll be completely safe," Lydia said firmly. "Surely, Clement will let us in —for the sake of Ditus."

"Clement? The jailer?"

"Yes. He's Ditus' friend. He won't refuse my request."

Pyrus shook his head. "I don't know, my lady. The position of jailer is a very —very difficult one. If he disobeys the orders of his superiors, if his prisoners escape, he'll be put to death. By torture and in deep disgrace."

"You mean you think he won't take Paul and Silas out of the stocks?" she asked in a small voice. "And Nuba?" she added quickly.

"I doubt it, my lady. He might—he just might let you give them some food. But surely that can wait until morning."

"No." Lydia was very decisive. "Tonight. I feel it's something I have to do."

"Then I'll go with you, my lady. But I confess that I can't really approve."

"Nevertheless, we'll go."

They were silent then, hurrying along the dark streets. Thoughts tumbled in painful chaos through Lydia's mind. In the middle of her memories of Valleius' anger and Fulvia's unexpected support, there came the quick realization that she had hardly even thought of Reuben as he deserved to be thought of. I should be grieving, Lydia thought. Oh, not hopelessly as I grieved for Aurelius, but with the sorrow Reuben merits. Only I don't have time. I promise, she pledged silently in her mind. I promise that as soon as I can be alone in my room, I'll mourn with decency.

I never even thought of leaving him all alone, she remembered with quick anguish. Hard on the heels came the comforting thought that Miriam would see to it. Miriam and her friends—maybe even the little "Rebekkah"—would keep watch by the old man's body with proper and dutiful respect.

For now, Lydia thought, I have to concentrate on Paul. He's the one who needs me. Reuben will never need anyone, ever again.

Luke and Timothy were inclined to agree with Pyrus about Lydia's going to the jail. They had already been there, they told her, and they were not even allowed to go near Paul and Silas. Why would things be any different for her?

"Did Clement know who you were?" she demanded.

"Yes. He just kept saying he had his orders."

She hesitated for a few seconds, thinking hard. It was

right for her to go. Somehow she knew it. But she would achieve nothing if Clement remained adamant. Maybe Ditus could persuade him.

"Is Ditus in his room?" she asked.

"I heard him go out after we came back in," Luke said.

"Well, if Ditus isn't here to send, then I'll have to go," she decided. "I can ask Clement to be understanding, to be lenient."

"I don't think—" Timothy began, but Lydia interrupted.

"I have to go. I *have* to. Pyrus, have you got the food, the wine?"

"Yes, my lady."

"Then we'll go. Come on."

They were silent, crossing the dark city. Their lamps made wavering, shifting splotches of dull gold on the pavement and reflected softly from Lydia's cream-colored stola and the blue and brown robes which Luke and Timothy wore. I ought to be terrified, Lydia thought, but I'm not. Either I really am sheltered and protected by Reuben's faith or my brain is numb from all the terrible things that have happened. I just can't seem to feel anything at all.

The jail, attached to the garrison, was a darker shape against the dark, star-patterned sky. There was a light in one window, but the thick walls prevented any sound from coming out onto the street.

"That lighted room must be where Clement stays," Lydia announced in a low voice. "He may not be alone. There are usually people with him, I'm told."

"Your son among them?" Luke asked, his voice as soft as hers.

"Yes, my son among them."

If Ditus is there, Lydia thought, he could be angry, embarrassed or resentful. She hadn't even thought of how Ditus would feel.

"It's too late now," she said abruptly.

"Too late for what?" Luke asked.

"To go back," she said. "Come on. Let's go in."

The room was full of men. There was talk and laughter, but through it all, Lydia heard the strong, vibrant sound of Paul's voice singing hymns.

"Isn't there any way to silence your prisoner?" someone yelled from across the room.

"No, no way." Clement's voice was abrupt. There was a strained look on his face, Lydia realized in the few seconds before he saw her. Something had upset him.

"Would it be possible to speak to the jailer?" Luke asked above the uproar.

"Alone," Lydia added firmly, and the room was suddenly quiet at the sound of a woman's voice.

There was a gasp. A flick of her eyes showed Lydia that it was Ditus who had reacted with such astonishment. If I don't acknowledge him, Lydia thought, perhaps he can pretend he doesn't even know me.

Clement stood up. "You wanted to see me? What about?"

"I'd like to talk to you without an audience," Lydia insisted. "Is that possible? Is there a room where we could go?"

"Yes." Clement limped toward a door that opened onto a long, narrow hall. "Come this way, please. You men go on with your game," he called back. "Maybe you'll drown out the sound of the prisoners."

Without looking to see what Ditus was doing, Lydia and her friends followed Clement down the hall.

Clement limped down several steps, and the sound of Paul's singing grew louder. Clement shook his head as though he were annoyed by stinging insects.

"I've learned to not hear groans and cursing. I never had to listen to this kind of man before."

His voice was only an irritated mutter, but Lydia, being closest to him, heard him clearly.

"That's because you may never have met a man like him before," she suggested.

"What is it that you want, Mistress Lydia?" Clement asked. "I've been forced to listen to preaching on the nature of God ever since I came on duty, so I must warn you that my patience has been sorely tried already."

"I only ask permission to take food and wine to Paul and Silas and Nuba," Lydia began.

"Nuba?" Clement raised his eyebrows in astonishment.

"The black slave. He's down there, too, isn't he?" she asked.

"He is. I think he's one of the ones they're preaching to. But why, in the name of all the gods, should *he* matter to *you*?"

Lydia saw a movement at the door and avoided looking in that direction, but she knew that Ditus had followed them and stood waiting.

"Because he's been hurt. Because he's innocent. Because he matters as much in the sight of God as you —or I," she said firmly, astonished at the ease with which the words came into her mouth.

"I've already told these men they can't see the prisoners," Clement said with a wave toward Luke and Timothy.

"But I thought because you knew me, you might make an exception," Lydia said, allowing a pleading note to come into her voice.

"I never make exceptions," Clement said shortly.

"Never?" Lydia said as her eyes looked directly into Clement's. She knew they were both remembering the night he had left his post to take a beaten and bloody boy to his home.

"Never!" The word was chopped off with defiance.

"Paul's not a young man," Lydia cried. "He won't be

able to bear this. He needs ointment on his cuts, wine and food to strengthen him. So do Silas and Nuba. We won't touch their bonds. I promise. Just let us give them some comfort."

Clement looked at her, and for a second it was as though there were only the two of them in the room. "I wish I could," he said gently, "but my punishment for failing to carry out orders would be death. Would you have me put to death just to make someone a little more comfortable?"

She stared back, and she knew he was right. She couldn't be instrumental in sending this man to his death, not even for Paul. If what Clement was doing was harsh and wrong, it was only because he saw it as his duty.

She felt tears begin again. Would she never be able to stop crying? There was just no way to get Paul out of the dreadful situation he was in.

"Don't cry," Clement said roughly, but she realized that there was tenderness in his eyes. "This God of yours—the one Paul's been talking about—why don't you ask him to help you?"

"Oh, I have, I have," she wept.

Suddenly the floor seemed to tilt and shudder. Lydia felt as though the earth were dissolving under her feet.

"Earthquake!" someone shouted.

There was the sound of stone rattling on stone and Lydia groped frantically for someone or something to hold on to.

"Get down," Clement shouted. "Get down!"

Lydia's mind was too tired, too bewildered to react. She only stood staring at Clement in the swinging light of the hanging lamp. Then the lamp was blown out, and she felt Clement's arms around her and the weight of his body as he pushed her to the floor and lay over her protectively while the small room was filled with the crashing, shattering sound of falling stones.

23

The dreadful heaving of the stone floor seemed to go on and on, although Lydia knew that probably only a few seconds had gone by since Clement had pushed her down and thrown himself protectingly over her. She lay limply, her mind dull and stupid, listening to Clement's breath rasp in and out. The man was apparently terrified, but it never occurred to her that his terror might be due to the fact that he thought her stillness was unconsciousness.

The floor was still shuddering when Clement, choking from the dust that filled the air, struggled to his knees to shake her shoulder.

"Are you all right?" he gasped. "Please speak to me. Are you all right?"

She opened her mouth to answer when a final heave of the earth seemed to lift the heavy edifice from its foundations. There was a clattering sound like an avalanche, and Lydia heard the dull crunch of stone against flesh and bone. Clement crumpled, his inert weight crushing her to the floor.

Instantly, her apathy disappeared. A raw, unexpected terror possessed her, giving her a strength that she had not known she had. She pushed and shoved until she was free of Clement's weight, only vaguely aware that she was scraping her arms and legs on the rough stone floor.

Struggling to her knees, she ran her hands over Clement's back and shoulders, feeling blindly in the darkness. Her fingers moved across the back of his head until they met the wet stickiness of blood.

"Clement's been hurt," she said in a clear, loud voice, heedless of anything but her discovery. "Can anyone find a light?"

"Mother, where are you? Are you all right?" It was Ditus, his voice strained and shaking.

"I think so. Are you?"

Her calmness was abnormal, she thought. She ought to be screaming and struggling, scrabbling to get out of this room where at any minute more rocks might fall.

"Yes," Ditus said. "Keep talking so I can find you."

"I'm here, with Clement. Wait, let me see if he's breathing. . . . His head is hurt. He must have been hit by one of the stones. . . . I'm here Ditus. Over here."

All the time she was talking, she was struggling to turn Clement's head, to find his lips so she could determine whether he was breathing.

She heard the other men calling each other, recognized Luke's and Timothy's voices, and knew a sense of gratitude that they were unharmed. But her greatest concern was for the man in her arms.

She found Clement's eyes—closed, thank God—didn't that mean he was unconscious rather than dead? She ran her fingers down to his nose and mouth and felt with relief the soft, damp movement of his breathing.

"He's alive," she cried, and she was astonished to find that Clement's breath on her fingers had started a wild hammering in her chest. Now she was afraid. Now she felt a terrible urgency to get Clement and the others out of this room and into the open. "Ditus, help me. Come and help me."

There were voices from the hall and in only a second, a soldier came to the door, holding a small lamp.

In the feeble light, Lydia saw only one thing, the condition of Clement's head. There was a bad cut, she realized, but she was grateful to see that there were no signs of shattered bone. Perhaps the damage was not as bad as she feared.

Ditus was kneeling beside her. "Bring the light," he called. "Clement's hurt. Here. Over here."

The soldier came across the room. "Is he dead?" he asked.

"No, only hurt. Here, take his legs. One of you take the lamp to lead the way. I'll take his shoulders. Come on, let's get him out of here! This is an outside room and might have been weakened. Come on, Mother. Follow me. Quick!"

Lydia saw the way the men hurried to obey Ditus, accepting his orders naturally. Here was no awkward boy but a young man to be respected and obeyed. Without question, she struggled to her feet to follow her son.

Luke was directly ahead of Lydia as they started out the door of the little room.

"I need another light," he said. "I've got to try to find Paul."

Paul! Lydia stared at Luke with horror. She had completely forgotten Paul during the past few minutes.

"The dungeon might be buried in rocks," she whispered.

Luke looked very grim. "A light," he called with authority in his voice, and surprisingly, someone provided a lamp for him. In the confusion, no one seemed to know who was really in charge.

"This way," Luke said tensely to Timothy. They turned to the right while Ditus and the others carrying Clement went toward the barracks room.

Without any hesitation, Lydia started to follow Luke. When he saw her, he stopped.

"Hadn't you better go out with Ditus?" he said. "This might be dangerous. There could be other tremors, you know."

"Paul's my guest," Lydia said firmly. "I came down here to help him. Reuben thought I should."

Luke didn't hesitate. "Then come on. But stay close to me—hold on to my robe.

Lydia didn't bother answering. She gritted her teeth and clutched Luke's robe. She didn't even think of the danger involved. This was simply something she had to do.

They had gone only a short distance when an unexpected sound met them. Paul and the others were singing—singing joyous, strong, affirmative hymns of praise.

"Listen!" Lydia gasped.

"It's Paul," Luke shouted. "And Silas. They're alive."

"Paul!" Timothy cried. "Are you all right?"

"We're safe," Paul shouted back. "All of us. Silas, Nuba, and I. And all the other prisoners. We're safe—and we're free."

"Free?" Lydia said. "What does he mean by that?"

"I don't know," Luke answered. "But here's the door." His fingers groped at the latch. "Look! It's open! The bolt's broken. Wait, let me shine my light."

Lydia, still clutching Luke's robe, stumbled on the uneven floor. In astonishment, she stared at the broken bolt and then looked beyond, into the dungeon. At first she could see nothing, only moving shadows; but as Luke advanced cautiously across the room, the rays of the lamp began to pick up the details of the scene before them. Paul, Silas, Nuba, and a dozen other prisoners stood, freed of their bonds, released from the stocks.

"What happened?" Lydia cried.

"God released us," Paul announced in a strong, confident voice. "There wasn't anyone killed in the earthquake, was there?"

"I don't think so," Lydia faltered. "We don't know anything about what happened outside the prison. Clement was hurt."

Paul smiled. "You'll find no one else was even hurt. You'll find that no other building was really shaken. This was God's work."

Hearing a stir behind her, Lydia glanced around quickly to see that two soldiers had followed them, holding another light. Their mouths were open in astonishment, their eyes stretched wide.

"You can escape," Luke said quickly to Paul. He obviously had not seen the soldiers. "While there's so much confusion, you can all escape."

But if the prisoners escape, Clement will be tortured and killed, Lydia thought with despair.

"Luke, Luke," Paul said, shaking his head. "Would God perform a miracle that would end in tragedy for the jailer? Have I taught you so little that you still think I would use a dishonest method to carry out God's will?"

When Lydia turned to assure the soldiers that Paul meant what he said, she discovered that they were gone. Their light was already so far up toward the upper hall that she knew they would not possibly have heard Paul's refusal to escape.

"We've got to get back to Clement," she gasped. "Those soldiers have gone back to tell that the prisoners are free. What if Clement is awake? He'll kill himself before he'd submit to the shame of —"

Paul spoke with quick determination. "You're right, Lydia. Hurry. Timothy, take the lamp and help her. Luke, stay here. And, Lydia, *run!*"

Lydia grabbed the lamp from Luke and thrust it into Timothy's hand. "Come on," she panted. "Hold my hand so we won't fall."

They raced up the steps together as though they were both Timothy's age. In only a minute they had reached the room where all the men were gathered and where several lamps had been lit. Clement, who had evidently been lying on a couch against the wall, was trying to struggle to his feet.

"Free?" he choked. "You say they're free? Give me my sword! Give it to me!"

Ditus tried to quiet the man, but Clement was obviously beyond the reach of reason or logic.

"I said give me my sword," Clement shouted. The blood smeared on his face made him look grotesque, but Lydia could see the bleakness in his eyes.

As one of the soldiers turned to obey Clement's command, Lydia threw herself on the man to imprison his arm.

"No," she cried. "Don't give it to him. Wait!"

The young soldier elbowed her away roughly and turned to hand the sheathed sword to Clement.

"No," Lydia screamed. "Wait!"

Clement looked at her and then spoke in a gentle voice. "Believe me, my dear," he said softly. "It's better this way."

His hand was steady as he drew the sword from the sheath and started to life the weapon so that its sharp, glinting point was aimed at his chest.

24

Ditus was frozen with horror, Lydia noticed. But Ditus didn't know that Paul and Silas and the others were still safe in the dungeon. Only she and Timothy knew that. Timothy was trying to shout something, but the voices of the frightened soldiers drowned him out.

Clement's hand tightened on the clasp of the sword, and she saw the muscles of his arm bulge. I can't make myself heard in this clamor, Lydia thought. There is absolutely nothing I can do. I'm helpless—unless God gives me his own power.

At that instant, a hush filled the room. Each man was suddenly silent, some mouths still holding the shape of the shouting. Lydia felt God's support and love as vividly as she had felt them at the moment of her baptism.

Her voice was low, clear, and strong. "The prisoners are safe, Clement. They have *not* escaped."

His hand shook, and the sword wavered as his fingers went slack. Timothy took immediate advantage of Clement's confusion and tore the sword from his hand.

"She's right," Timothy said, his voice as calm and quiet as Lydia's had been and as clearly discernible. "She's absolutely right. Not a prisoner has escaped."

Clement looked bewildered. "But the soldiers said they were freed from the stocks," he began.

"Yes, freed from their stocks," Lydia said, "but they are honorable men of God. They're still there. Come and see."

Clement shook his head, his eyes dazed. "There's no man living who wouldn't try to escape if he could."

"Come and see," Lydia urged again.

"My mother may be right," Ditus said. "This Paul—he's not an ordinary man, Clement."

The jailer looked at Lydia and Ditus. "I'll go and look," he finally agreed. "But I demand that my sword be given back to me.

When Timothy handed the sword to Clement, Lydia felt a little spasm of fear. Clement was surely dazed and confused from his head injury. It was possible that he might not trust his senses even when he saw Paul and the others in the dungeon.

"This Paul," Clement said thickly, as his hand strayed up to touch his head. He pulled his fingers away and looked at the blood on them. "This Paul—what he's been saying about his God ever since they brought him in—can it possibly be true?"

Ditus looked sharply at his mother as though he were warning her not to speak. Even as recently as a day ago, she might very well have kept her convictions to herself. But Reuben had bequeathed her his faith, and God had guided and upheld her all through the events of this night.

"Yes," she said sturdily to Clement, ignoring Ditus' warning glance. "Everything Paul has been saying about God is true. It's *true!*"

"They will have escaped by now," one of the soldiers cried. "These two were probably sent up here to create more confusion."

"We'll go and see," Clement said in a toneless voice. He was obviously dizzy and swayed a little as he started to walk. Ditus took his arm to steady him, and Lydia dropped back to follow humbly. She was surprised to discover how badly she wanted to be the one to walk with Clement and equally surprised to discover how easy it was, all at once, to turn things over to Ditus. She should have known that Ditus was capable of doing anything he really wanted to do. Well, she knew it now, she thought as she picked her way around the rubble that cluttered the floor, and she was ready to step down and turn the shop over to him. She'd tell him if they ever got safely out of here.

At the foot of the steps leading into the dungeon, Clement and Ditus pushed ahead of the others to come face to face with the prisoners.

Lydia was too far back to see what was happening, but she heard Paul's voice ring out with a strong command. "Do yourself no harm," he cried, "for we are all here."

There was a long silence, and then Lydia heard the clatter of metal on stone and realized that Clement had dropped his sword onto the floor. Two of the soldiers in front of her moved apart and she was able to see, in the flickering light, that Clement was kneeling in front of Paul. Kneeling! Clement!

His voice was broken and humble. "Sirs, what must I do to be saved?" he said.

Lydia's eyes blurred with sudden tears, and when she was able to blink them away she saw a sight that was, to her, even more astonishing than Clement's actions. Ditus was also kneeling in front of Paul, and his face, in the lamp's light, was marked with something almost like adoration.

"Yes," Ditus said, his voice a young and vibrant echo of Clement's words. "What must I do to be saved?"

Paul's glance flickered over to Lydia before he spoke to the two kneeling before him. There was triumph on his face and joy and a tenderness she had never seen before. When he spoke, he spoke to Clement, but his hand was resting on Ditus' head. "Believe in the Lord Jesus," he said. "Only believe and you will be saved —you and your household."

"Then we should be baptized," Clement said struggling

to his feet. "As I have heard you explaining to the other prisoners earlier."

"You're badly hurt," Paul said. "Let Luke bathe and stitch
your wound."

"Not down here," Clement said. "The prison may not
even be safe. You will all come to my house —every one of
you." His sweeping gesture took in the entire group.
"Since there won't be any prisoners here, I'll be free to
leave my post. Come on." He swayed a little and turned
humbly to Luke. "If you'll staunch the blood first? I'm getting weak."

"Paul could heal you," Ditus said.

Lydia stared at her son in astonishment. Was this the
Ditus who had always denied his own miraculous healing?

"Not I," Paul said sternly. "I never healed anyone in my
life. Only God can heal. Luke can fix up this kind of hurt.
With you, my boy, a greater power was needed."

Ditus smiled, and Lydia was surprised to see Paul's face
soften in an answering smile. "Some day," Paul promised,
taking Ditus' arm and leaning on it for the ascent of the
stairs, "some day, you'll be a comfort and a strength to me.
When you're older, when God's time is right."

"In the meantime," Lydia heard herself saying clearly,
"until you need him, sir, you must let him stay with me to
take over the business that's rightfully his."

Ditus' face was a blaze of glory, and Paul's eyes were
warm with approval. "A good decision, my friend," Paul
said to Lydia. "While the boy makes a success of his business, you will help me build the church."

Dawn was paling the eastern sky before anyone began to
think of leaving Clement's house. Paul had preached to and
questioned his new converts, and Syntyche, Clement's
married daughter, had served fruit and wheat cakes and
glasses of wine. Hymns had been sung, and Lydia had
been quietly joyful, watching the expression on Ditus' face

and seeing the color slowly come back to Clement's cheeks.

"But it's nearly morning now," Lydia said finally to Paul. "We must leave and get ready for this day. There's so much to do. We have to make arrangements for Reuben's funeral —"

The look on Paul's face stopped her. "Reuben?" he said.

"Oh, I forgot that you wouldn't know. Reuben —died last night." Her voice shook badly.

"A wonderful old man," Paul said warmly. "A blessed old man who followed the Law and walked with his God and who came to know the Lord Jesus Christ. What a glorious day this must be for him."

"But I'll miss him," Lydia said.

"Of course. If you choose to."

"Isn't it normal to feel sad?"

Paul shrugged. "It's normal to feel sad and normal to feel happy. These are minor things. The important thing is to feel the spirit of God in you so that sadness and happiness are both part of his glory."

"I sometimes wonder if I'll ever really understand," Lydia said.

"Perhaps. Perhaps not. But never stop trying."

"If *she* must keep trying," Clement said, coming up to where Lydia and Paul stood together, "what of us who know nothing?"

"You'll study and grow," Paul said. "It's no different for me. I still fall short of the glory of God and do things which I ought not to do. We're all children, you know."

"Tired children," Lydia dared to say in a mildly joking tone, "who need some rest. What are you going to do, Paul? What ought I to do?"

"I'm going to stay here," Paul said. "In the safest room I can find."

"What if Valleius orders you put in stocks again?" Lydia asked, feeling cold at the thought.

"If that's God's will for me," Paul said, "then I'll go back into the stocks. I can't believe that will be his will. Would he release me for nothing?"

"I'm frightened," Lydia admitted.

"Don't be afraid," Clement said. "I'll see that Paul is all right. Even if he's put back in prison, I'll make sure he's comfortable and warm."

"But the power of Valleius," Lydia began.

"Lydia!" Paul's voice was sharp. "When will you learn that you can trust God? You do some things that persuade me that you really believe, and the next minute, you're worrying and trying to foresee every possible future condition."

She stood chastened. "I'm sorry," she whispered.

Clement smiled at her. "We'll learn together, shall we?" he said.

She nodded and was ashamed at how quickly her heart was eased.

"Are you ready, Mother?" Ditus came up to her, and his face was solicitous. "You look tired."

"I'm very tired," she admitted. "Will you take me home?"

"Don't worry," Paul said. "Everything will work out."

"And I'll see you soon?" Clement asked in a low voice.

She looked up into his face and knew with great certainty that her answer was terribly important. "Soon and often, I hope," she replied quietly without glancing at either Ditus or Paul. Her eyes looked steadily into Clement's.

"Thank you." His slow smile warmed his eyes, and for just a second she caught a glimpse of the gentleness and sweetness that had been hidden by the grief he had suffered and the grim work he did. Someday, that gentleness might be shared with her, and she might be happier than she had ever dreamed of being again.

Lydia returned the smile and, taking Ditus' arm, turned to leave the room. A sharp knock at the door started everyone into an uneasy silence.

"Valleius!" Lydia's lips formed the name as she looked with fear into Ditus' face.

A young soldier threw open the door, disclosing several policemen on the step.

"Yes?" The soldier's word was terse, but his hands knotted with tension.

"We were sent from the Magistrate Valleius," one of the policemen said, and Lydia felt her heart jerk with fear. "The—the strangeness of the earthquake in the prison area—when none of the rest of the town was shaken—has led the magistrates to—to alter their decision about the Jewish prisoners."

No one in the room moved. Every figure might have been carved out of stone, Lydia thought. The silence was so deep that even all breathing seemed to be suspended.

"The prisoners are to be released," the policeman announced unexpectedly.

Lydia felt relief and joy wash over her in a wave. She looked at her son and saw that his eyes were as bright as hers must be.

"Did you hear that?" she whispered.

Ditus nodded, and they both turned eagerly to see Paul's reaction to what was surely another miracle from God.

But Paul was looking at the policemen with a cool, disdainful expression.

"These magistrates have sent policemen to release us? But if we refuse to go, what then?" he said.

There was a general gasp of disbelief, and the faces turned toward Paul were filled with amazement.

"They had us whipped in public," he said, "and then thrown into jail. We who are Roman citizens!"

Again there was a gasp of astonishment, and Lydia found herself almost unable to breathe.

"And they sent you secretly to discharge us secretly?" Paul went on, the words hard and precise. "No! That's not the way it's going to be!"

"But you never said you were a Roman citizen," one of the policemen protested.

"Didn't I? How do you know? If you were there, would you have been able to hear me over the crowd? I tried to say the words—but no one listened."

Lydia remembered Paul's lips shaping words just before the whips lashed down. He was right, of course. No one could have heard even if Paul had tried to tell them.

"Have you proof?" the second policeman asked.

"Would I be so foolish as to make a claim I couldn't prove?" Paul asked coolly. "No, go and tell the magistrates that they have whipped Roman citizens and thrown them into stocks without trial. A public apology *may* keep me from taking my complaint to Rome. I'm not sure."

The policemen stared with bewilderment around the room and then turned to hurry away from the prison. There was silence for a minute.

"A Roman citizen?" Clement asked, almost in a whisper.

Paul smiled grimly. "A Roman citizen," he agreed. He turned to Ditus and spoke urgently. "Take your mother home and make her rest. Unless I'm very much mistaken, Valleius is going to wish he had never heard of Saul of Tarsus."

Feeling lightheaded from the way event had piled upon event, Lydia walked without speaking along the streets of Philippi in the pale morning light.

It was Ditus who finally broke the silence. "Did you mean it?" he asked.

"Did I mean what?"

"What you said about the business?"

"I only wonder," she said in absolute honesty, "why I waited so long."

Ditus stopped to stand, looking at her with an expression of delight. "Thank you," he said at last.

"Don't thank me." Her voice caught and then steadied itself. "I just want you to know one thing. I made up my mind to do it *before* you were baptized. When you showed what kind of man you were when Clement was hurt, I knew then. Can you believe me?''

He nodded without speaking and then, oblivious of the people on the street, he bent his head and kissed her with love.

25

Lydia, Minta, and Ditus sat on a sunny bench in the peri-style, having a little breakfast and exchanging the news of the tumultuous night that had just passed.

"There wasn't any earthquake here," Minta said, round-eyed. "I hardly slept at all after David brought me home, so I would have known. I know that sometimes there are quakes which affect only small areas, but what happened last night doesn't seem normal. Does it?"

"Well, it wasn't normal," Ditus said. "It was obviously a miracle."

Minta stared at her brother with amazement. "What did you say?" she gasped.

"I said it was a miracle." But Ditus' eyes were glinting with laughter as he looked at Minta.

"Does he mean it?" Minta begged, turning to her mother. "Does he mean miracle in the way *we* mean miracle?"

"Yes." Lydia knew that her eyes must be shining with the peace that filled her. "He means it. Paul baptized him last night."

"Oh, Ditus!" Minta cast herself into her brother's arms. "I've never been so happy in my life." She hugged him rapturously and then drew herself away with a somber expression. "How can I say that—about being so happy, I mean, when Reuben is dead and Paul is still in prison?"

241

Lydia looked at her daughter and was slowly conscious of a great truth. "I think sometimes we have to be happy on faith," she said, groping for the words. "I have a hard time with this. Paul has lectured —no, scolded —me twice about it. I seem to think I have to have a positive answer for everything before I dare let myself relax and enjoy it. But sometimes we have to let God handle things."

"How do you do that?" Ditus asked. "How do you *know* what God wants you to do —or even that what God wants is what will make you happy?"

"I don't know." Lydia's voice was solemn. "I guess it's a matter of accepting the things you can't change —of asking constantly for His guidance —of feeling right when you're doing what's right."

"Did you feel right about turning the business over to me?" Ditus asked.

"I haven't felt so right about anything since your father died," Lydia said. She turned to Minta. "Don't look so astonished. I've enjoyed being a businesswoman. I've been proud of doing what had to be done. But Ditus—Epaphroditus—is a man now."

"We haven't had the coming-of-age ceremony," Minta began doubtfully. "What about offering gifts to the Roman gods? You know we couldn't do that. And Ditus doesn't even have a sponsor."

Ditus' face brightened. "Mother! *I* know! Paul can put the toga pura on me. He's a Roman citizen!"

"But Paul won't approve of the ceremony," Lydia began.

"Of course not," Ditus said. "I don't approve of it now myself. But we can make our own ceremony —something very simple —with an offering to the one true God."

The boy's eyes were blazing, and Lydia felt a sudden premonition. Some day God would call this boy away into a life of danger. "What kind of an offering?" she asked, but she knew what his answer would be.

"An offering of me," Ditus answered simply. "Some day

—not now because I have work to do and much to learn—
but some day, I will follow Paul and serve him and God.
Couldn't the offering be me?"

Lydia nodded. "I'm sure," she said slowly, "that God
would count it worthy."

Kora came into the room. "My lady, there's a slave at the
door. One of the Tatinius slaves. He refused to give me the
message, said he must speak directly to you."

"I'll see to it," Ditus answered.

"Yes, do," Lydia said. A sudden thought struck her. "It
might be a message from Fulvia, Ditus. If it is, I'll come.
She may have really insisted that only I receive it."

Ditus nodded and strode briskly toward the atrium.

"He's different," Minta said. "He really is."

"My lady," Kora interposed anxiously. "You look exhausted. You're not going to the shop today, surely?"

"I may not go very often at all in the future," Lydia said.
I'm making Ditus head of the shop, and I'll go only when
he really needs me."

Kora's sigh of relief was almost laughable. "Oh, my lady,
you mean you'll be home sometimes —giving orders again
and making decisions? That's the most wonderful news
I've heard in a year."

Lydia stared at her slave with astonishment. "You mean,
I've really made life that difficult for you? I'm sorry, Kora."

"It's my duty to do what needs to be done," Kora said
primly, but the elation in her eyes denied the tone of her
voice.

"Mother." Ditus came back in. "You're right. It's a message from Fulvia. For your ears alone, the man says, and he
acts as though he's scared to death."

Lydia got up stiffly, feeling pain and fatigue in every part
of her body. This was how it would feel to be old, she
thought. No wonder Reuben wasn't dismayed at the
thought of dying.

Foolish thoughts, she scolded herself. She should be

thinking only of what Fulvia's message would be. But, in a way, wasn't it a sign of her new faith that she could think of something that had no bearing on the present concern? Perhaps.

The slave stood well inside the door and constantly darted looks over his shoulder toward the street.

"My lady," he said with relief when Lydia appeared.

"Your mistress has sent me a message?"

"Yes. She wanted me to tell you that the Magistrate Valleius is planning to go to the prison about midmorning. She —Mistress Fulvia —is not sure what he plans to do. But she thought you ought to know."

"Thank you," Lydia said. "Tell her I'm grateful —and, wait! Also tell her that Reuben's funeral will be held at dusk today. There's no time to do it sooner. Will you tell her that? Even if she's not able to come, I want her to know."

"Yes, my lady." One more frightened glance over his shoulder to ascertain that the way was clear, and the slave was gone.

"I hadn't even thought of Reuben's funeral," Lydia confessed to Ditus, who had come back into the atrium. "Not until just now. Will it be all right to wait until dusk?"

Minta had followed Ditus. "Yes," she offered. "Miriam saw to it that the coin was placed in his mouth, the spices put on, and the burial sheet wound around him. I —I helped."

"You?" Lydia asked in astonishment.

"Yes. I knew you had to be where you were, and it seemed that I should do what I could. It didn't seem awful —to touch him, I mean. I just kept reminding myself that the part of Reuben that really mattered was already gone."

Her chin quivered and her eyes filled with tears. Lydia put her arms around Minta and held her close. "It seems that both of my children are grown up all at once," she said. "I'm proud."

"What are we going to do about Fulvia's message?" Ditus asked. "Do you want me to go to the prison?"

"No, you hurry to work," Lydia said. She caught herself and added swiftly, "Don't you agree that's the better way? Clement is at the prison to support Paul, and I'll go there as soon as I've had time to clean up and change my clothes."

"Ought you to?" Ditus asked. "It's you that Valleius wants to hurt, not me."

"It's what I have to do," Lydia said with quiet confidence. "Don't worry. God will take care of me."

Ditus stared at her searchingly, and what he saw seemed to reassure him. "All right," he said. "I'll go to the shop then, but at noon I'll come to the prison to see how things are going."

"If we're not there," Lydia said, "Come look for us here."

"I envy you your faith," Ditus announced.

It was what I once said, Lydia thought, but faith was something that grew, it seemed, something that could be shared. Without the help of Reuben, Fulvia, and Paul, her own faith would still be thin and tenuous. Perhaps, in time, she could give to Ditus what had been given to her.

Kora brought a basin of warm water, and Lydia washed herself quickly. Her body longed for the comfort of the baths, but she had no time this day for luxury. Under Kora's loving and skillful hands, the well-groomed, attractive woman she usually was began to emerge. Watching the mirrored reflection of Kora's deft hairdressing, Lydia let her mind drift back to that which she had, until now, held in abeyance—the thought of Clement. What, exactly, had been revealed in that brief flash of tenderness when he had looked at her? How disheveled, weary, and sorrowful she must have looked, and yet he had appeared to find her lovely. And to what had she committed herself when she had said she hoped to see him soon? Was she ready to love again?

"Kora," she said, breaking the silence. "Paul isn't married. Nor are Luke and Timothy and Silas. Have you felt that Paul thinks marriage is wrong?"

"Not wrong, my lady," Kora said, intent on her work, "but perhaps not necessary. If Jesus comes back soon, then people won't need marriage, I guess. Do you think that's what Paul's been implying in some of the things he's said?"

All these years Kora's wisdom and perception had been there, hidden under the rigid wall between slave and master, Lydia thought. How lovely that Paul's teaching had crumbled the barrier of tradition.

"Perhaps," Lydia agreed slowly. "But what if one wanted to marry?"

"I'm only a new convert," Kora reminded her mistress. "But —I would think it would all depend on what condition would let you serve God best. As a married woman, could you do more for the followers of Jesus than as a widow?"

Lydia made no effort to pretend that she had been discussing generalities. "There would be less talk," she said in a low voice, "less talk about people coming here if there were a master of the house. Ditus could serve, of course, but —"

"But Ditus is young and will probably want his own house someday," Kora declared. "It's not good for a woman to be alone."

Lydia dropped her eyes and looked at her hands. Could it possibly be the will of God that she should serve him and still know joy and fulfillment? Shouldn't one face sacrifice for one's faith?

Kora spoke softly. "Paul said once that the Lord Jesus told his followers that he had come that they might have a more abundant life. I think it's something to remember."

"Thank you, Kora." Lydia reached up and touched Kora's hand. "There! I look all right now. Ask Pyrus to come, will you, and we'll go back to the prison."

"I'm —I'm frightened, I think," Kora admitted. "I wish you didn't have to go."

"Don't be afraid. I know God will be with me, no matter what happens. While I'm gone, will you see that the house is freshened and that flowers are taken into Paul's and Silas' rooms? They'll need some beauty after the desolation of the prison."

"Are you so sure they'll be back, my lady?"

"I suddenly seem to be sure of everything," Lydia said quietly.

She was halfway across the city when she felt a strong conviction that she ought to stop at the shop first. Ditus will think I'm interfering, she tried to tell herself, but the conviction would not go away. If God is going to speak to me, I must listen, she reasoned, and headed for the shop.

She reached the opening of the stoa and was about to step inside when she heard Valleius' voice.

"Where's your mother?" he demanded.

Ditus' voice was smooth and confident. "She's home, resting. But she may be going out soon. She has much to see to —the release of Paul, Reuben's funeral —"

"Why isn't she here?"

"The business has been turned over to me," Ditus said. "I plan to spare her as much of the problems of the shop as I can."

There was a silence. When Valleius spoke, his voice was ugly. "Turned the business over to you? A child?"

"I'm seventeen tomorrow, sir," Ditus said sturdily. "A man in the eyes of Roman law. But you know all aspects of Roman law, of course."

There was a subtle threat in the last words. Ditus was daring to remind Valleius that the Roman law was not to be trifled with and that Valleius had already erred seriously in his false arrest of Paul and Silas.

"A brave boy," Pyrus whispered to his mistress.

"A brave man," she whispered back. "Come. I don't want them to know I'm here."

She hurried down the street, armed and strengthened by the conversation she had overheard. Ditus' courage was contagious, and she realized that she was no longer afraid of Valleius or of what he might do.

26

Valleius is coming," Lydia announced as soon as she reached the prison. "I think he's on his way here now."

Paul looked up from the chair where he was sitting. He had been leaning forward, resting on his elbows, his eyes closed, his face etched with weariness and pain.

"Valleius is no danger," Paul said. "He has broken the Roman law. He has no choice but to apologize."

"To you, perhaps," Lydia said. "I wonder how it will be with me. Not that I'm as worried as I was," she added hastily, watching the approval warm Paul's eyes.

There was a stir at the door, and they all turned to see Valleius and his fellow magistrate standing in the opening.

"I sent policemen to release you," Valleius announced in a stiff, hard voice. "Why haven't you left the prison?"

"You had us whipped publicly," Paul returned. "You had us thrown in jail without a trial. You broke the law of Rome that says that every Roman citizen deserves a fair trial. And then you expected me to creep out secretly at dawn —perhaps even endangering the life of the jailer. You underestimate me."

Valleius' face was an ugly red. "Well, I'm here to publicly release you. Now, leave and get out of our town."

"And the jailer?" Paul asked coolly.

Lydia's heart jerked.

"He's not my responsibility," Valleius admitted reluctantly. "The military is its own authority. If he hasn't deserted his post or lost a prisoner, he's probably blameless."

"You heard that?" Paul turned to the soldiers who stood in the room.

They nodded their heads. "Yes, sir."

Paul got stiffly to his feet. "Then, with your permission, my friends and I will leave."

"Stop!" Valleius said roughly. "Nuba isn't a citizen of Rome. He stays here."

Compassion filled Paul's eyes. He turned to Nuba and put his hand on the dark arm. "Don't despair, my son. We'll pray for you."

Nuba's face was serene. "It's all right. I've had more joy in the past few days than I ever expected to have in my life. I've been treated as a man. I've been shown the way to God."

"I treated you as a man," Valleius shouted. "I gave you more freedom than you deserved. As for this nonsense about God, we'll see if he's great enough to get you out of prison."

Nuba looked steadily at his master. "Yes, my lord," he agreed. "You gave me more freedom than many masters would have. And I abused it by helping Erosa escape. Whatever you decide, my lord, will be only just."

Everyone stood in stunned silence at the honesty and courage Nuba had demonstrated. If God can do *that* to a slave facing prison, Lydia thought humbly, I don't think I'll ever question his power again.

Valleius' eyes wavered and slid away. "Put him in the dungeon," he said roughly to one of the soldiers. "Just in chains. Not in stocks."

"The stocks are all broken, sir," the soldier replied.

Valleius' head jerked and his nostrils had a pinched look. He's frightened, Lydia thought. I've never seen him frightened, but he knows something bigger than himself has been at work here.

"See to it that they're repaired," Valleius barked, turning away.

The soldier took Nuba's arm, but without harshness, Lydia saw. The slave smiled at them all and allowed himself to be led from the room. This was what Reuben had meant so long ago when he spoke of his own troubles. Life wasn't suddenly perfect even for those who believed. But if one had faith, God would provide the strength that was needed.

"Can we go now?" Lydia begged Paul.

At the sound of her voice, Valleius wheeled around. "What are you doing here?" he demanded.

"I'm just waiting to see that my guests are free to come to my home," she replied steadily.

Valleius glared at her, but she returned his look without wavering. She really wasn't afraid of him, she discovered. She had been so terrified that he would ruin her business, destroy her reputation, and hurt her friendship with Fulvia that her cowardice had been a crippling and destructive thing. Valleius needed a seller of purple in Philippi —Fulvia had told her that long ago —and as angry as he might be, he would not find it to his advantage to really discredit Aurelius' business. As for her friendship with Fulvia, Valleius had been warned long ago by Erosa that he wouldn't be able to change that. It was true. It was really true.

"You haven't heard the last of me," he muttered.

She felt only a sensation of serenity, knowing her lack of fear had rendered him helpless. It was her terror that had given him a sense of power.

"I'll pray for you," she said soberly as Valleius turned on his heel and stamped away.

"You're learning," Paul said with great satisfaction. "When we leave Philippi, I won't have to worry about my young church. I know that Lydia and Clement and Epaphroditus will hold it safe and strong."

His words reminded her of something he had said the

first day he came to her house. "You thought your visit to Philippi would be a comfort for your soul," she said, "and instead, it has been a time of trouble and difficulty for you."

Paul shook his head. "No, you're wrong. There has been no persecution toward the building of a church, no difficulties with the Jews in the town, no bitterness or quarreling among the new converts. I'll always think of Philippi with love."

Lydia smiled at Paul as she turned to lead the way out the door. It was then that she saw Clement standing across the room. His head was turbanned with bandages, but his face was calm.

"Tomorrow," she said breathlessly to Clement, "when the sun rises, we'll celebrate Ditus' coming of age. Will you come?"

Clement grinned with the old look of confidence. "And would I miss it? The boy is like a son to me."

She felt a sudden spurt of joy. "Till morning, then," she whispered, then hurried out the door.

The funeral at sundown was simple. David had dug a grave, and Reuben's body was lowered into the earth with reverence and respect.

"Surely this day," Paul quoted, "you shall be in paradise."

Lydia felt the tired tears slipping down her face. There was no bitterness in her, none of the angry futility and terrible aloneness that she had felt a year ago. There was only loneliness, a sort of homesickness which hurt but which could be borne.

"Amen," the people said.

Paul had forbidden professional mourners, the wailing and the rending of garments. "Let him go in peace," he had announced. "In peace and with hope."

Hope. A strange word for a funeral, Lydia would have said once. Now, it seemed the only word to use.

They walked together in the blue twilight toward Lydia's house. The heat of the spring day had given way to a cool breeze, and Lydia felt the freshness of it drying her tears. She held Ditus' arm, grateful that he was meansuring his steps to her weariness.

"Minta's in love with David," she found herself saying in a confiding tone to her son. She hadn't even known she was thinking about it. The words had just come out.

Ditus nodded. "Of course. Could it be otherwise?"

"He's poor," Lydia murmured. "They'll never have much. She has no father to give her a dowry."

"She has a brother," Ditus announced. "She'll be rich with love and God's care. What more can you want for her?"

"Nothing." Lydia's voice reflected her deep feeling of content. Why hadn't she known that Ditus would take care of everything?

"Speaking of marriage," Ditus said apologetically, "we couldn't really afford it, but this afternoon I offered Valleius such a high price for Erosa that he swallowed his pride and accepted it. I hope you don't mind."

"There wasn't anything else to do," Lydia said. "She couldn't have hidden at Miriam's forever."

They walked in silence, and the meaning of Ditus' words hit her. "But what has that to do with marriage?" she asked.

She felt Ditus' shoulders move in a shrug. "Perhaps nothing. I may never marry. I don't know how God will lead me. But if I ever do, well —" His voice trailed off.

"Thank you for telling me," Lydia said humbly. "She's very beautiful."

"And very young," Ditus added, his voice suddenly merry. "There's lots of time yet." His next words were so sudden that Lydia jumped. "I expect we have to think about you and Clement before we think of either Minta or me."

"Clement and me?" Lydia faltered.

"I'm not blind," Ditus said calmly.

"And to think," Lydia said in a wondering voice, "that I wasted this whole year thinking of you as a child."

Ditus laughed. "Part of the time you were right. Is that a comfort to you?"

She nodded without speaking. There were no words to express the peace that filled her.

The level rays of the rising sun struck through the open door of the peristyle and cast sharp shadows across the clipped grass. The pool reflected the tender blue of the morning sky, and Lydia found that she was trembling as Ditus walked toward the center of the room.

"I've no patience with the usual Roman tradition," Paul had said the night before when she approached him with her request that he sponsor Ditus' coming of age. "But — perhaps in this case — and if we use it as a time to dedicate the boy to God —"

"It's what he suggested," Lydia urged.

"Then I'll do it. This once."

Now, Paul stood in the center of the peristyle, the simple white toga, the toga pura, spread across his hands. Ditus came close to Paul, and Lydia saw for the first time how much the boy had grown. Paul had to tip back his head to look into Ditus' face.

"I declare you, Epaphroditus, son of Aurelius, a man — in the eyes of the law and of God," Paul said, his hands deft and gentle putting the toga over Ditus' head and draping it about his shoulders. "I give you, with all your strengths and weaknesses, into God's care and keeping. You will be his man from this day on."

Ditus' face was very pale, but his eyes were blazing. "From this day on," he pledged, "I will serve God and his Son, Jesus the Christ, with all my strength and all my heart."

Paul smiled. "The Lord bless you and keep you," he said, and Lydia's heart tightened as she remembered the sound of Reuben's voice saying the same words. "The Lord make his face to shine upon you and be gracious unto you. The Lord lift up his countenance upon you and give you peace."

Lydia's hand groped for Minta's, and she felt the warm strength of the young fingers in hers. Oh, God had blessed her beyond her rashest dreams in giving her children like these.

She felt her other hand being taken in a firm grip, and turning, she looked into Clement's eyes. It was the first time he had ever touched her so, and she was astonished at the way her heart began to race. In only a few seconds, the racing had settled down to a strong, steady beating that gave her a sense of comfort and security. What had she done to earn this lovely sense of God's blessing, she wondered. Glancing up, she found Paul looking at her. She knew what he would say if he could read her mind. She hadn't *earned* anything. There was no possible way to earn God's grace. It was a gift given with love and could only be received with gratitude.

"In the name of Almighty God," Paul said, turning again to Ditus. "And of his Son, our Lord Jesus Christ, and of the Holy Spirit. Amen."

Lydia looked with brimming eyes from her children to Clement, to Paul, Silas, Luke, and Timothy, to the slaves who stood on the edges but who, within the circle of love, were friends that with her would build the church of Philippi.

"Amen and amen," Lydia said, feeling the hands holding hers tighten, hearing the echo of the people around her. "Amen and amen."